Hiding Behind The Cross

D. Elias Loadholt Sr.

Published by Living Water Publishing, 2025.

HIDING BEHIND THE CROSS

First edition. June 1, 2025.

Copyright © 2025 D. Elias Loadholt Sr..

ISBN: 979-8231552061

Written by D. Elias Loadholt Sr..

To my beautiful children,**Cyarrah, Savannah, and Dwayne Jr.**

You are my heart in three parts.Your strength, your light, your laughter, and your love inspire me every single day.May you always walk in truth, stand in purpose, and know that God has placed greatness inside of you.

This story is for you—to remind you that healing is possible, faith is powerful, and grace will always find us.

I love you more than words will ever say.

— Dad

"Sometimes, we don't need to be rescued from the storm—we need to be reminded that God still sees us in the middle of it."—D. Elias Loadholt Sr.

Chapter 1: The Calling

1   The year was 2013, and twenty-four-year-old Raymond Johnson was about to deliver his first sermon at a small church in Georgia. The late spring air was warm and thick, almost stifling, as he paced the tiny room that served as a pastor's office. His heart raced with a mix of excitement and nerves. He ran his hands over his suit, worn but well-kept, a gift from his mother, who had saved for months to make sure her son looked like a proper man of God.

Raymond heard the murmurs from the sanctuary—a crowd of maybe thirty people, some leaning forward in their seats with anticipation, others sitting back, arms crossed, skeptical of the young preacher they'd heard so much about. But one person's presence mattered more than any other: Pastor Williams. His mentor, a man of deep faith and conviction, had been the first to see Raymond's potential, pulling him from a wayward path and guiding him toward the ministry.

As the choir finished a rousing rendition of *Amazing Grace*, Raymond took a deep breath and stepped into the sanctuary. The pulpit loomed before him, a modest wooden stand that had seen decades of sermons, weddings, and farewells. Raymond gripped its edges, grounding himself, and gazed out at the faces watching him.

"Brothers and sisters," he began, his voice trembling slightly before finding strength, "we're here today to remember that no matter how lost we feel, God sees our worth. We're here because we believe in redemption."

As he continued, Raymond felt his nerves dissolve. His voice grew steady, the words flowing as if he were a conduit, a mouthpiece for a message that wasn't his own. He spoke of forgiveness, of the power of faith, and of God's unyielding love. It was a message as old as time, but in that moment, it felt as fresh and personal as the sweat on his brow.

By the end of his sermon, he saw tears in the eyes of some of the congregants. He had reached them. And as he stepped down from the pulpit, Pastor Williams approached, pride evident in his eyes.

"You've got something special, Raymond," Williams said, clasping a hand on his shoulder. "But remember, it's not just about the sermons. A man of God must live the Word, even when it's hard."

Raymond nodded, feeling a weight settle in his chest—a weight of responsibility, of calling. This moment would stay with him for years, a constant reminder that faith wasn't just spoken; it had to be lived.

2

Ten years later, Pastor Raymond Johnson stood at the pulpit of Rhema Word Tabernacle in Brooklyn, New York, looking out over a congregation of nearly a thousand. At twenty-nine, he was the youngest pastor in the Rhema Church network, and whispers had already begun about his potential for a bishopric. But prestige was the last thing on his mind.

Today was an unseasonably warm March Sunday morning. Sunlight streamed through the stained-glass windows, casting colorful patches across the sanctuary. The energy in the room was electric, filled with the hum of voices and the scent of incense. As Raymond walked down the center aisle, his congregation rose to their feet, honoring him as they always did.

"Turn with me in your Bibles to Isaiah, chapter fifty-four," he said as he took the pulpit. "Let's read verse seventeen together: 'No weapon that is formed against thee shall prosper.'"

The congregation echoed his words, some already breaking into shouts of praise. Raymond smiled, holding up a hand. "Now, now, let me give you my subject before y'all start to shout."

His voice rose, filling the room, resonating with the deep conviction that had only grown in him over the years. "People of God, I want you to know that no matter what the enemy tries, he cannot stop you, nor can he block you."

He preached with a fervor that was born of experience and faith, taking his congregation on a spiritual journey. For the next twenty-five minutes, his voice rang out, rising and falling with emotion, guiding them through a message of resilience and divine protection.

When the sermon ended, the congregation descended from their spiritual high, many wiping tears, others clapping and shouting their thanks. Raymond felt a deep satisfaction, but as he stepped down, he knew his work was far from over. Behind the admiration of his congregation, he felt an emptiness, a lingering shadow of loneliness and doubt.

As the service drew to a close, he made a few brief announcements. "Just a reminder," he said, "we're hosting Pastor Joseph Marston and New Hope A.M.E. at 5 p.m. today. Let's all be back on time. Praise and Worship team, be in place. We're building a culture of consistency."

Consistency had been Raymond's mantra, especially for his congregation. Over the past four years, he had drilled it into them, determined to change the perception that the Pentecostal church was unorganized or casual about time. He believed that if they showed respect for their time, they would be able to reach more souls.

As he closed the service with a benediction, his security team gathered his Bible and briefcase, ready to escort him back to his office. He walked through the crowd, stopping to greet members as he went.

"You blessed my soul today, Pastor," said Sister Jenkins, the head of the Mother's Board. She clasped his hand, her eyes filled with admiration.

Raymond smiled warmly. "Thank you, Mother Jenkins. Your support means more than you know."

Finally, he reached his office, closing the door with a sigh of relief. He instructed his head of security to give him thirty minutes alone before he began his counseling sessions. He leaned back in his leather chair, scanning the room. His office was a reflection of his taste—plush carpeting, mahogany desk, and bookshelves lined with theological texts. But despite the luxury, he felt a strange discontent, as if all the material success in the world couldn't fill the void inside him.

Raymond rose, heading into the small, marble-tiled bathroom adjacent to his office. He stripped off his charcoal-gray suit, drenched in sweat, and stepped into the shower. As the water cascaded over him, he whispered a prayer. "Lord, I thank you for using me today. I know I am nothing but an unclean vessel, but thank you for your faithfulness."

The words trailed off, and he felt a sudden surge of emotion, his tears mixing with the water. No matter how many people he reached, how many souls he saved, there was an aching loneliness within him—a sense that something vital was missing.

Raymond finished his shower, dressing in a sharp, black suit for the evening service. He was just fastening his cufflinks when there was a knock at the door.

"Pastor, Sheniqua Lewis is outside. She wants to see you," said his head of security.

Raymond took a deep breath. "Send her in."

Sheniqua was a sixteen-year-old girl who had been attending Rhema Word with her mother for years. Raymond had made a commitment to support the youth of his congregation, especially since he had been given his pastoral role at a young age. Sheniqua entered, her face drawn and troubled.

"What can I do for you, Sheniqua?" he asked, his voice gentle.

She sank into the chair across from him, tears brimming in her eyes. "Pastor, I can't take it anymore. I have to get out of my house."

Raymond listened as she poured out her frustrations with her mother, her voice wavering between anger and despair. She spoke of feeling stifled, of the constant demands and expectations that left her feeling unseen.

"Sheniqua," he said softly when she finished, "I know you're going through a lot. But remember the first commandment with a promise: 'Honor thy father and mother, that thy days may be long upon the earth.' It doesn't mean life will be easy, but God has a plan for you."

She sniffled, nodding reluctantly. "I understand, Pastor."

As she left, Raymond felt a pang of empathy. He remembered being her age, struggling to balance his own dreams with the expectations of those around him. But he also knew that, unlike him, Sheniqua had no one to lean on, no mentor to guide her through the storms of youth.

3

The evening service at Rhema Word Tabernacle was in full swing, the sanctuary alive with worship as the choir sang a powerful medley of *We've Come This Far by Faith* and *Victory Is Mine*. Raymond Johnson sat quietly in the second row, his Bible resting on his lap. For the first time in a long while, he wasn't leading the service—he was simply there to receive.

Tonight's guest preacher was Pastor Joseph Marston from New Hope A.M.E., a respected minister and close friend. Raymond had invited him months earlier, believing the congregation could benefit from a fresh voice. As much as Raymond loved preaching, he recognized his need to be fed spiritually—a need he rarely acknowledged aloud.

Pastor Marston ascended the pulpit with practiced ease, greeting the congregation warmly. His commanding voice resonated through the sanctuary as he read from Isaiah 54:17: *"No weapon that is formed against thee shall prosper."*

The congregation erupted with shouts of *"Amen!"* and *"Preach, Pastor!"* Raymond found himself nodding in agreement, the familiar Scripture stirring something deep within him.

Marston continued, his words cutting through the air with precision. "People of God, the enemy's plan has always been to make you believe you're defeated. But I came to tell somebody tonight—*you're still standing!"*

Raymond closed his eyes, letting the words settle in his spirit. He could feel the truth of Marston's message pressing against the unresolved heaviness he carried—burdens he rarely spoke of, even in prayer.

4

By the time the sermon ended, the sanctuary was electric with praise. Tears streamed down faces, hands stretched toward the heavens, and spontaneous shouts of *"Thank You, Lord!"* filled the air. Raymond remained seated, head bowed, lost in his thoughts even as the congregation rose to their feet.

He stayed still until he felt a gentle touch on his shoulder. Opening his eyes, he saw Mother Jenkins, her face glowing with a mix of reverence and joy.

"That word was for you too, Pastor," she said softly. "Even you need reminding sometimes."

Raymond managed a faint smile, nodding as she returned to her seat. He appreciated her sincerity, but the ache in his chest remained.

5

After the service, Raymond lingered near the altar, watching as congregants prayed in small groups or sought personal counsel from the ministry team. He noticed Sheniqua Lewis standing alone near the back, her expression unreadable.

Before he could approach her, Pastor Marston appeared at his side. "You alright, Ray?"

Raymond forced a smile. "I'm good. Powerful word tonight."

Marston studied him for a long moment, seeing through the practiced facade. "You know, sometimes even the shepherd needs tending."

Raymond sighed, nodding slowly. "I guess I forget that sometimes."

"Don't let the work consume you," Marston urged. "God called you to lead, but He didn't call you to do it alone."

Their conversation was interrupted by the head of security signaling that the church doors were being locked for the night. Raymond shook Marston's hand firmly.

"Thank you again for coming."

"Anytime, brother. And remember—you're not just a preacher. You're a man who needs grace too."

As Marston departed, Raymond turned back toward the altar, finding it empty now—just polished wood reflecting the soft glow of the sanctuary lights.

He walked slowly to the front, resting his hands on the edge of the pulpit, allowing himself to feel the full weight of the day. His whispered prayer rose into the stillness:

"Lord... refill me. I'm running on empty."

The silence that followed was deafening—but strangely, it felt like the beginning of an answer.

Chapter 2: The Ice Begins to Melt

1 Shannon Walker-Johnson moved through the bustling offices of Thompson Walsh Securities, heels clicking against the polished floors. Heads turned as she passed, not because of her striking appearance—though she was undeniably beautiful—but because of the aura of confidence and professionalism she exuded. She was the first African American woman to hold the title of Vice President in the company, a role she had fought for and earned through years of relentless dedication.

But today, despite the congratulatory nods and friendly greetings from her colleagues, Shannon felt a weight pressing down on her—a heaviness that had nothing to do with work. She paused at her office door, glancing at the nameplate that read "Shannon Walker-Johnson, VP of Marketing." The name was hers, yet it felt foreign, as if the person she had become was worlds apart from the woman who once stood beside Raymond at the altar, vowing a lifetime of love and partnership.

As she settled at her desk, her phone buzzed with a reminder of the lunch meeting she had almost forgotten. Robert Miller, a senior executive at Thompson Walsh, had invited her for a casual lunch to "talk shop," but Shannon suspected there was more behind his invitation. Robert had been kind, supportive—even charming at times. But every time he hinted at something beyond friendship, Shannon felt a wall rise within her, cold and impenetrable.

It wasn't that she didn't like Robert. He was good-looking, successful, and attentive. He was everything a woman could want, everything her family encouraged her to find in a partner. But every time she considered the possibility of a relationship, she felt a pang of guilt, a tether to the past she hadn't fully severed.

The pain of her last relationship hadn't faded, nor had the love. Raymond had been the center of her world, a man of conviction and charisma, but their marriage had unraveled in ways she still struggled to understand. She blamed herself at times, then him, then circumstances beyond their control. Yet no matter how many times she dissected the past, she couldn't find a way to let it go.

2

Lunch with Robert took place at an upscale restaurant not far from her office. As they settled into their seats, Robert flashed her his easy, warm smile. "It's good to see you outside the office, Shannon. Sometimes, I feel like we're always in a boardroom."

She laughed, forcing herself to relax. "I suppose that's the nature of the beast. The higher you climb, the more the walls seem to close in."

Robert nodded, his gaze lingering on her. "Shannon, you're an incredible woman. I've admired your dedication, your work ethic, your strength. But I feel like there's a lot about you I don't know."

Shannon looked down at her glass, swirling the water in it absently. "There's not much to tell. Work has been my life for a long time."

"But it doesn't have to be that way," he said softly. "You deserve to be happy, outside of work. To have someone share the load, if you're open to it."

His words stirred something within her—a reminder of the life she'd once had, the love she had shared, and the heartache that had followed. But she couldn't imagine opening up again, not yet, not when the past still held her so tightly.

"I appreciate that, Robert," she replied, her voice gentle but guarded. "But right now, I'm just focusing on what's in front of me."

The rest of their conversation drifted back to work, the easy camaraderie they both enjoyed. But as they parted ways, Shannon felt a hollow ache. She wanted to move on, to open her heart again, yet a piece of her remained chained to Raymond, to the life they had built and lost.

3

That evening, Shannon sat alone in her apartment, the city lights casting a dim glow across the room. She held a glass of wine, staring at the photograph on her mantle—a picture of her, Raymond, and their daughter, Keturah, taken on a bright summer day before everything fell apart. The laughter in their eyes, the joy that once felt unbreakable, seemed like a distant memory.

Her thoughts drifted back to the day she had walked away, leaving behind the love and the pain, the dreams and the heartbreak. She had tried to forget Raymond, to erase the hurt, but he lingered in her thoughts like a ghost. She thought of Keturah, who looked so much like her father, and wondered if her daughter, too, carried traces of his spirit, his faith, his warmth.

Unable to bear the silence any longer, she knelt beside her bed, her hands clasped in prayer. "Lord, I don't know what I'm supposed to do. I thought I could move on, that I could let him go. But something is holding me back. Help me to forgive, to release this pain. Show me the way forward, even if it's without him."

Her words felt hollow, but they were a beginning. She knew that forgiveness was the only path to peace, yet it was a journey she feared. In that moment, Shannon realized that the love she had for Raymond hadn't died. It had merely been buried beneath layers of bitterness, waiting for the day when she might finally let it see the light again.

4

The following Sunday, Shannon attended her father's church, Tribe of Levi Tabernacle, where she was scheduled to sing a solo. She had chosen a song that resonated with her heart, *I Won't Complain*, a hymn that had comforted her through countless sleepless nights. As she took her place at the front of the sanctuary, she felt a surge of strength.

The first notes left her lips, soft and trembling, but as the song swelled, so did her voice. She sang with a power that was as much about resilience as it was about faith, pouring her heart into each verse. The congregation rose, hands lifted, voices joining her in praise.

When she reached the final line, her voice cracked with emotion. Tears streamed down her cheeks, a mixture of pain and release. She felt the eyes of the congregation on her, a witness to her vulnerability. Her father, Bishop Walker, stood nearby, his face filled with pride and understanding.

After the service, Shannon sat in the pew, her heart full. Her younger sister, Tasha, joined her, nudging her playfully. "Girl, you sang like you were trying to bring down heaven."

Shannon laughed, wiping away the last of her tears. "I think I needed it more than anyone else."

Tasha's smile faded, her gaze turning serious. "You've been carrying a lot, Shannon. And I know you're strong, but even the strongest people need a break."

"I know," Shannon admitted. "It's just... hard to let go. To forgive."

Tasha placed a hand on her shoulder. "Maybe forgiving Raymond isn't about letting him off the hook. Maybe it's about freeing yourself. You've built this amazing life, sis, but there's more out there for you. And I think it starts with forgiveness."

Shannon nodded, feeling the weight of her sister's words. That night, as she lay in bed, she felt a flicker of hope. Perhaps it was time to let go, to release the hold that the past had on her heart. She didn't know what the future held, but for the first time, she felt a glimmer of possibility—a chance to love again, to heal, and to find peace.

5

The following week unfolded in familiar rhythms: meetings, deadlines, and power lunches at Thompson Walsh Securities. But something felt different within Shannon—subtle yet undeniable. Her father's sermon and her sister Tasha's words lingered, touching corners of her heart she had long closed off.

Late one evening, she sat in her office, the glow from her computer casting soft shadows on her face. The building was quiet, most employees having left hours ago. She stared at the marketing proposal on her screen, but her mind was far from work.

Her fingers hovered over the keyboard before she minimized the document and opened a new email window. For a moment, she considered reaching out to an old friend—someone outside her professional world—but quickly dismissed the idea. Vulnerability was still unfamiliar territory.

With a sigh, she closed her laptop, grabbed her coat, and headed toward the elevator. As the doors slid shut, she let out a breath she hadn't realized she'd been holding.

6

That Saturday, Shannon decided to clear her mind with a walk through the city's botanical gardens. The air was crisp but not too cold, and the faint scent of blooming flowers hinted at spring's approach.

She wandered along the winding paths, letting the quiet beauty soothe her restless thoughts. She stopped near a small koi pond, watching the fish glide gracefully through the water. Their effortless movement made her think about how often she fought against the current of her life, struggling to maintain control.

What if I just... let go? she wondered.

A soft breeze tugged at her coat, making her shiver. As she turned to leave, her phone buzzed in her pocket—a text from her best friend, Camille Turner.

Camille: *Brunch tomorrow? My treat. We need to catch up!*

Shannon smiled for the first time all day. Camille had been a constant in her life, someone who saw through her walls and loved her anyway.

Shannon: *Absolutely. 11 a.m. at Marlowe's?*

Camille: *Done! Can't wait!*

Tucking her phone away, Shannon felt a hint of warmth settle in her chest—a small reminder that she wasn't as alone as she often felt.

7

Sunday brunch with Camille was just what Shannon needed. The cozy bistro buzzed with soft conversations and the clatter of dishes as they settled into a corner booth.

"You're glowing," Camille teased, studying her over the rim of her coffee cup. "New promotion? Secret admirer?"

Shannon laughed, shaking her head. "Neither. I guess... I'm just trying to find some balance."

Camille raised a skeptical eyebrow. "*You?* Balanced? The woman who schedules downtime like it's a board meeting?"

Shannon smirked. "I'm working on it."

Camille reached across the table, squeezing Shannon's hand. "I'm glad. You've been through so much... you deserve to breathe again."

For the first time, Shannon didn't argue or brush off the sentiment. Instead, she let herself believe it—if only for a moment.

8

Later that evening, Shannon curled up on her living room sofa, a soft blanket draped over her legs as she flipped through old photo albums. She hadn't meant to pull them out, but something about her conversation with Camille had sparked a longing she couldn't ignore.

She traced her fingers over a picture of herself holding a two-year-old Keturah at the park, both of them laughing as if the world held nothing but joy. Her heart ached with the memory, but there was no bitterness this time—only a wistful yearning for the innocence of that moment.

I can't change the past, she reminded herself. *But maybe... I can stop running from it.*

With that thought, she set the album aside and reached for her journal. The words came slowly at first but soon spilled onto the page with surprising ease:

"Lord... thank You for not giving up on me, even when I gave up on myself. Help me learn how to trust again... how to love... how to forgive."

Her hand trembled as she closed the journal, feeling a strange lightness in her chest—a small but undeniable crack in the ice she had built around her heart.

Chapter 3: A Heart Reborn

1 Tasha Walker sat in the waiting room of the prenatal clinic, one hand resting protectively on her growing belly. She glanced around at the other women—some accompanied by husbands or partners, some alone but content. A quiet envy pricked her heart as she watched a couple across the room laugh together, the man reaching over to squeeze his wife's hand. She quickly looked away, focusing instead on the new life within her, the child she would raise on her own.

The nurse called her name, and she stood, taking a steadying breath. This was her third visit, but each time felt like a reminder of the path she had chosen—the path she had been forced to walk alone. Yet as much as she wished things were different, she knew that she would never regret her decision to keep the baby. Her son had become her reason for resilience, a light in the midst of a dark season.

As she lay on the examination table, her doctor smiled at her. "You're doing great, Tasha. Strong and healthy. And so is your little one."

Tasha returned the smile, feeling a flicker of pride. She was doing this, one day at a time, creating a life for her son—a life filled with love, even if it lacked the traditional family she'd once envisioned.

But as she left the clinic, a thought nagged at her. She had gone from feeling anger toward Walter to, strangely, feeling nothing at all. He had been absent for months, and while she told herself she didn't need him, there were moments, late at night, when the hurt resurfaced.

She wondered if he even thought about them—if he cared, if he felt regret.

"Not today," she whispered to herself as she stepped onto the bustling Brooklyn street. "Today's not the day for that."

2

That evening, Tasha sat in her parents' living room, her father's church sermons playing softly in the background as she sifted through the baby clothes her mother had been collecting. The air was filled with the warm scent of the casserole her mother had cooked, and the ambiance was cozy, almost like a balm for her spirit.

"Tasha, honey," her mother, Katherine, called from the kitchen, "come taste this and tell me what you think."

Tasha rolled her eyes playfully. "Mama, I'm eating for two now. You know I'll eat just about anything."

Katherine laughed as Tasha joined her in the kitchen, sampling the casserole. As she ate, Katherine placed a gentle hand on her shoulder. "You're going to be an incredible mother, Tasha. This baby is already so loved."

Tasha swallowed, the warmth in her mother's words nearly bringing tears to her eyes. "Thank you, Mama. I just... I just wish I could give him more."

Katherine's face softened. "Sweetheart, love is more than enough. This child will have a family who loves him unconditionally, who will teach him strength and faith. You don't need anyone else."

Tasha nodded, feeling her mother's words settle over her like a comforting blanket. But as they worked side by side, folding baby clothes and sharing stories, Tasha's thoughts drifted once more to Walter. Her father's sermon played in the background, and she heard the words about forgiveness, about the importance of releasing resentment for one's own peace.

As much as she wanted to move forward, a part of her wondered if she would ever be able to forgive Walter, or if holding onto the hurt was her way of staying strong.

3

The following Sunday, Tasha sat alone in the pew at her father's church, Tribe of Levi Tabernacle, as the congregation filled the sanctuary with worship and praise. Her father, Bishop Walker, was in his element, his voice resonating through the church as he delivered his sermon on forgiveness.

"For we wrestle not against flesh and blood," he preached, his voice booming with conviction. "Forgiveness isn't for the other person. It's for you. It's the key to freedom, the release from chains you didn't even know you were carrying."

Tasha shifted in her seat, her gaze fixed on her father as he spoke. She felt the weight of his words pressing down on her, each one challenging the anger she had clung to for so long. She had heard sermons about forgiveness her entire life, but today, they felt different—closer, more personal, as if they were meant just for her.

After the service, she lingered in the pew, watching as the congregation filtered out. Her father approached, his usual stern demeanor softened as he looked at her.

"Baby girl, you doing alright?" he asked, his voice tender.

She managed a smile, but her eyes betrayed her inner turmoil. "Daddy, I'm trying. I want to let go of the anger I feel toward Walter, but every time I think I'm ready, it just... it hurts all over again."

Bishop Walker placed a gentle hand on her shoulder. "Tasha, forgiveness doesn't mean you have to forget what he did. It doesn't mean you have to welcome him back. It simply means you're freeing yourself. Holding onto anger only hurts you."

Tasha took a shaky breath, her father's words resonating in a way they hadn't before. "Maybe I can try," she whispered, almost to herself. "Maybe... for my own peace."

Her father squeezed her shoulder. "Take your time, baby girl. Forgiveness is a process, not a moment."

4

Later that week, Tasha received an unexpected call from Walter. She stared at her phone, his name flashing across the screen, her heart pounding. She had thought about this moment so many times, imagining what she would say, how she would respond. But now that it was here, she found herself frozen.

Taking a deep breath, she answered. "Hello?"

"Hey, Tasha," Walter's voice was low, almost hesitant. "I know it's been a while. I... I wanted to check in on you and the baby."

She held the phone tightly, resisting the urge to let her anger spill out. "You're a little late for that, Walter."

He sighed on the other end of the line. "I know. I've been doing a lot of thinking, and I realize I was wrong to walk away. I want to be involved, Tasha. I want to help."

Tasha felt a surge of frustration, her mind racing with memories of his absence, of the nights she'd spent wondering if he even cared. "And what changed, Walter? You didn't want to be a part of this months ago. Why now?"

There was a pause, a silence filled with unsaid words. "Because I was scared, Tasha," he admitted, his voice barely above a whisper. "I thought I wasn't ready, that I couldn't handle it. But I realize now that I was wrong. I don't expect you to forgive me, but I want to try to make things right."

Tasha closed her eyes, struggling to keep her composure. She had waited for this moment, for this apology, but now that it was here, it didn't feel the way she had imagined. She wanted to believe him, to let go of her resentment, but a part of her remained guarded, unwilling to let him in so easily.

"Walter," she said, her voice steady, "if you want to be involved, you'll have to prove it. Actions speak louder than words. I'm not going to let you in and out of our lives on a whim. This isn't just about you anymore."

There was a moment of silence, and then Walter spoke, his voice soft but resolute. "I understand. I'll do whatever it takes."

As she ended the call, Tasha felt a strange mixture of relief and apprehension. She didn't know if Walter would follow through, but for the first time, she felt a sliver of hope that maybe, just maybe, they could find a way to co-parent in peace.

5

That night, Tasha sat in her bedroom, her hands resting on her belly, whispering a quiet prayer for herself and her unborn son. "Lord, give me the strength to forgive, to let go of this anger. Help me to find peace, for me and for my child."

As she spoke, a sense of calm washed over her, a peace she hadn't felt in months. She didn't know what the future held or if Walter would truly change, but she knew that she was ready to move forward, with or without him. She was ready to build a life of love, of resilience, and of faith.

And as she lay down to sleep, her heart felt lighter, her spirit renewed. This was her journey—a journey of forgiveness, of healing, and of the unbreakable bond between mother and child.

Chapter 4: The Burden of Leadership

1 Raymond sat alone in his office at Rhema Word Tabernacle, the weight of his responsibilities pressing down on him like a physical force. The once-bustling sanctuary had emptied after Sunday service, leaving an echoing silence that felt heavier than the presence of his congregation. The numbers from the church's latest financial report lay open on his desk, the figures swimming before his eyes.

It wasn't the first time he had faced a challenge as a pastor, but this crisis felt different. Rhema Word Tabernacle had grown rapidly over the past few years, its membership swelling to over a thousand. With growth had come increased expenses—more staff, larger facilities, expanded community outreach. But the tides of support had shifted, and tithes were down. The church was struggling to keep up with its obligations, and Raymond knew he couldn't ignore the problem any longer.

He had called a meeting with the church board for later in the week, but the thought of asking his congregation for additional support made him uneasy. He didn't want to burden them, especially when so many were already giving as much as they could. But what choice did he have? The alternative was to cut programs that served the very people who needed them most.

As he mulled over his options, his phone buzzed with a message from his daughter, Keturah. He felt a rush of warmth as he read her text: "Daddy, can we get ice cream after school tomorrow?"

He smiled, his troubles momentarily forgotten. Keturah was the light of his life, the one constant source of joy and purpose. But even as he looked forward to their time together, he felt a pang of guilt. His role as a pastor often left little room for fatherhood, and he worried that his dedication to the church was costing him precious moments with his daughter.

Taking a deep breath, Raymond texted her back, promising to meet her after school. He couldn't fix everything, but he could be there for Keturah. And maybe, just maybe, that would be enough for now.

2

The next day, Raymond arrived at Keturah's school just as the bell rang. He watched her run out of the building, her face lighting up when she spotted him. She raced over, throwing her arms around his waist, and he lifted her up, relishing the sound of her laughter.

"Daddy, can we get chocolate and sprinkles?" she asked, her eyes wide with excitement.

"Anything you want, princess," he replied, feeling a surge of gratitude for the simple joy she brought to his life.

They walked to a nearby ice cream parlor, Keturah chattering about her day, her friends, and a school project she was excited about. Raymond listened, hanging on her every word, savoring the moment. But as they sat down with their ice cream, he noticed a slight shift in her demeanor. She was quiet, her gaze fixed on her spoon as she swirled it in her bowl.

"Is everything okay, Keturah?" he asked gently.

She looked up, her expression hesitant. "Daddy, why don't you and Mommy talk anymore?"

The question hit him like a punch to the gut. He had tried to shield Keturah from the fallout of his divorce from Shannon, but he knew that children were perceptive. They sensed things, understood more than adults often realized.

Raymond took a deep breath, choosing his words carefully. "Sometimes, grown-ups go through things that make it hard to talk to each other. But that doesn't mean we don't both love you very much."

Keturah nodded, but the sadness in her eyes lingered. "I just wish we could all be together. Like we used to."

Raymond's heart broke a little at her words. He wanted to promise her that things would get better, that he and Shannon would find a way to be a family again. But he knew he couldn't make promises he might not be able to keep.

"I know, baby girl," he said softly, reaching across the table to take her hand. "And I'll always be here for you. No matter what."

They finished their ice cream in silence, but as they walked home, Raymond felt a renewed determination. He couldn't change the past, but he could work toward healing the wounds it had left. For Keturah's sake, and maybe even for his own.

3

That evening, Raymond returned to his office, preparing for the board meeting that would take place later in the week. He spread out the financial reports, the expense breakdowns, and the list of programs at risk. He couldn't shake the feeling of helplessness that had settled over him, a reminder that even men of faith sometimes struggled to find answers.

As he stared at the numbers, his thoughts drifted back to Shannon. She had been his partner in everything once, his confidante, his support. She understood the pressures he faced better than anyone, and there were times when he longed to reach out to her, to share his burden. But their separation had been painful, a wound that still ached despite the years that had passed.

He closed his eyes, remembering the moments they had shared—the laughter, the late-night talks, the dreams they had built together. He knew that part of the reason he struggled so much was because he had lost his support system, the person who had been his rock. And as much as he tried to deny it, he missed her.

A knock on his door pulled him from his thoughts, and he opened his eyes to see Deacon Henderson standing in the doorway, his expression serious.

"Pastor, may I come in?"

Raymond gestured for him to enter, mentally preparing for the difficult conversation ahead.

"Pastor," Henderson began, sitting down across from him, "I know you're worried about the church's finances. And I wanted to offer some suggestions."

Raymond listened as the deacon proposed a series of cost-cutting measures—scaling back outreach programs, postponing building renovations, and possibly reducing staff hours. Each suggestion felt like a small defeat, a reminder of the sacrifices that might be necessary to keep the church afloat.

"Thank you, Deacon," Raymond said, his voice weary. "I appreciate your input. But I'd like to hold off on any cuts until we've explored all our options. I don't want to turn our backs on the people who depend on us."

Henderson nodded, though his expression remained skeptical. "I understand, Pastor. Just know that we're here to support you, whatever you decide."

As the deacon left, Raymond leaned back in his chair, his resolve hardening. He didn't know how they would overcome this crisis, but he was determined to find a way that didn't involve abandoning their mission. He would pray, he would work, and he would trust that God would provide a path forward.

4

The week passed quickly, and before Raymond knew it, Sunday morning had arrived again. The sanctuary was filled with familiar faces, each one a reminder of the lives his church touched. As he stepped up to the pulpit, he felt the weight of his congregation's expectations pressing down on him, but he also felt a surge of faith, a conviction that they would find a way through this.

"Brothers and sisters," he began, his voice steady and clear, "today, I want to talk about perseverance. About holding onto hope, even when the road ahead seems uncertain."

He spoke of faith, of trust, of the power of community. And as he preached, he felt his own doubts begin to fade, replaced by a quiet certainty that they would overcome this together.

At the end of the service, he made a brief announcement about the church's financial needs, urging his congregation to pray and consider ways they could support the ministry. He saw the worry in their eyes, but he also saw resilience, a willingness to stand with him in this trial.

After the service, as he greeted members of the congregation, he felt a familiar presence by his side. He turned, surprised to see Shannon standing there, Keturah's hand in hers. She looked at him, her expression unreadable, and for a moment, the noise of the sanctuary faded away, leaving only the two of them.

"Shannon," he said softly, his heart pounding. "Thank you for coming."

She nodded, her gaze steady. "Keturah wanted to see you preach. And... I thought it was time."

They stood in silence, each struggling to find the right words. Finally, Shannon spoke, her voice barely above a whisper. "Raymond, I know things ended badly between us, but I think it's time we tried to move forward. For Keturah's sake."

Raymond swallowed, his throat tight with emotion. "I agree. She deserves to see us getting along."

They shared a tentative smile, a small step toward reconciliation. And as he watched Shannon walk away with Keturah, Raymond felt a glimmer of hope—a sense that, despite everything, healing might be possible.

5

That night, as Raymond sat in his office, he allowed himself a rare moment of vulnerability. He closed his eyes and whispered a prayer, asking for guidance, for strength, and for the courage to face the challenges ahead. He prayed for his congregation, for his daughter, and for Shannon. He didn't know what the future held, but he was ready

Chapter 5: Facing the Past

1 Shannon sat alone in her apartment that evening, staring at the city lights flickering outside her window. The sounds of Brooklyn pulsed in the distance, a constant reminder of the life she had carved out for herself, a life she had built from the fragments of her broken marriage. She had told herself for years that she was better off, that her career and Keturah were all she needed. But after seeing Raymond that morning, memories she thought she'd buried began to resurface.

Their interaction had been brief, almost formal, yet there had been an undercurrent of warmth, a familiarity that pulled at her heart. She hadn't expected it to feel this way—to feel like they were standing on the edge of something, something that could either heal them or tear them apart again.

Shannon's thoughts drifted to Keturah. She remembered the longing in her daughter's eyes whenever Raymond's name was mentioned, the quiet sadness that seemed to settle over her whenever she saw other children with both parents. Shannon had tried to be everything for her daughter—mother, father, friend. But there was a part of Keturah's heart that only Raymond could fill, and Shannon knew it was time to let that happen.

But what about her own heart? Shannon sighed, pressing a hand to her chest. Forgiveness was a word she'd heard her whole life, preached by her father from the pulpit, extolled in every hymn and sermon. But the reality of forgiving someone who had hurt her so deeply was more difficult than any prayer could ease.

2

The next day at work, Shannon buried herself in tasks, meetings, and deadlines. Yet, no matter how many emails she sent or presentations she rehearsed, thoughts of Raymond and their past lingered at the edge of her mind. She couldn't shake the feeling that she needed to confront the unresolved pain, the questions she had never allowed herself to ask.

During a rare lull in her day, she texted her sister, Tasha, asking if she could come over that evening. Tasha responded with a quick "Of course!" along with an enthusiastic emoji. Shannon smiled, grateful for her sister's unwavering support.

That evening, Shannon arrived at Tasha's apartment with a bottle of wine in hand. Tasha greeted her with a hug, her belly now showing the unmistakable curve of pregnancy. They settled on the couch, the wine poured, and for a moment, they sat in comfortable silence.

Tasha was the first to speak. "So... you and Raymond. I saw you two together on Sunday."

Shannon took a deep breath, staring into her glass. "It was... strange. We barely spoke, but just being around him brought back a lot of things. Good things, bad things."

Tasha nodded, her expression gentle. "That's normal. You two shared a lot. It's only natural for those feelings to come up."

Shannon hesitated, swirling her wine as she searched for the right words. "I keep telling myself I'm over it—that I've moved on. But seeing him again, it made me realize that maybe I haven't let go of everything. Maybe I haven't forgiven him."

3

Tasha leaned in, her tone soft. "Forgiveness isn't just a decision, Shannon. It's a journey. And maybe it's time you let yourself take that journey."

Shannon sighed, feeling the weight of her sister's words. "I don't even know where to start, Tasha. How do you forgive someone who broke your heart? Who shattered the life you thought you'd have?"

Tasha took a sip of her wine, her expression contemplative. "You know, I used to think forgiveness was about letting someone off the hook. But it's more about setting yourself free. It's like… when you forgive, you're releasing the hold the pain has on you. You're choosing to move forward, even if the scars are still there."

Shannon looked away, the thought both comforting and terrifying. "Sometimes I wonder if it would be easier just to keep things the way they are. To avoid him, to keep my distance."

"But is that fair to you? Or to Keturah?" Tasha asked gently. "She deserves to see her parents getting along, to know that she's loved by both of you."

Shannon nodded slowly, her heart heavy. "You're right. I know you're right. But I'm afraid, Tasha. What if I let go of this anger, and I realize there's still something between us? Something I can't ignore?"

Tasha gave her a sympathetic smile, reaching over to squeeze her hand. "Then maybe that's part of the journey too. Maybe forgiving him isn't just about moving on, but about seeing what's still there and deciding what you really want."

Shannon sat back, her mind reeling. She hadn't allowed herself to think about the possibility of rekindling anything with Raymond. The hurt had always felt too deep, the betrayal too raw. But now, as she considered the possibility of forgiveness, she felt a tiny flicker of hope—a hope that maybe, just maybe, the love they once shared wasn't entirely lost.

They spent the rest of the evening talking about other things—Tasha's pregnancy, work, family—yet Shannon felt a new clarity growing within her, a determination to face her feelings and confront the past. As she hugged Tasha goodbye, she whispered, "Thank you. I didn't realize how much I needed this."

Tasha smiled, her eyes warm. "You're stronger than you think, Shannon. And you deserve to be happy—whatever that means for you."

4

The next Sunday, Shannon found herself back at Rhema Word Tabernacle. She hadn't planned on coming, but something had drawn her back, a quiet pull she couldn't ignore. She took a seat in the middle of the sanctuary, her heart pounding as she looked around at the familiar faces and the vibrant energy of the congregation.

Raymond was at the pulpit, his voice strong and steady as he preached about resilience, about the power of faith to carry one through life's storms. She felt his words resonate within her, each one piercing through the walls she had built around her heart.

As the sermon ended, the congregation rose in applause, and Shannon joined in, her hands clapping slowly as she watched him. He seemed different today, lighter somehow, as if he, too, was carrying less of a burden.

After the service, as the congregation mingled and chatted, Shannon made her way to the front, feeling a strange mix of nerves and anticipation. When she reached him, Raymond looked up, surprise flickering across his face.

"Shannon," he said softly, a small smile forming. "I didn't expect to see you here."

She returned the smile, feeling her heart race. "I... I wanted to hear you preach. And to talk. If you're up for it."

Raymond's gaze softened, and he nodded, leading her to a quieter corner of the sanctuary where they could speak without interruption. They stood facing each other, the silence stretching between them.

"I've been thinking a lot about us," Shannon began, her voice barely above a whisper. "About what happened, and... and about forgiveness."

Raymond's face grew solemn. "Shannon, I know I hurt you. And I know that asking for forgiveness is a lot. But if there's anything I can do to make things right, I want to try."

Shannon looked away, gathering her thoughts. "It's not that simple, Raymond. Forgiveness isn't something I can just hand over. It's something I have to feel. And I'm... I'm not there yet. But I want to try. For Keturah. And maybe... maybe for us."

Raymond nodded, his eyes reflecting a mixture of hope and regret. "I understand. And I want you to know, Shannon, that I'm here. Whatever you need, whatever it takes, I'm here."

They stood in silence for a moment, each processing the weight of their words. Finally, Shannon extended her hand, her voice soft but resolute. "Maybe we can start over, as friends. For now."

Raymond reached out, taking her hand in his, a gentle smile touching his lips. "I'd like that."

As they left the sanctuary together, Shannon felt a sense of peace she hadn't known in years—a feeling that maybe, just maybe, the journey toward healing had truly begun.

5

Later that week, Shannon sat in her living room, watching Keturah play with her toys. Her daughter's laughter filled the room, a reminder of the joy that remained in her life, despite the pain and the struggles. For the first time, Shannon allowed herself to imagine a future where forgiveness was possible, a future where her heart might be open again.

As she knelt beside Keturah, helping her stack blocks, she felt a calm settle over her. She knew the road ahead wouldn't be easy, but she was ready to face it, step by step, day by day. And as she looked at her daughter, she whispered a silent prayer, thanking God for the strength to move forward and the courage to heal.

This was only the beginning, but it was a beginning she welcomed with open arms, her heart finally ready to let go of the past and embrace whatever the future held.

Chapter 6: Strength in the Storm

1 Tasha sat alone in her small apartment, her hand resting on her belly as she watched the rain trickle down the window. The steady rhythm of the rain was usually soothing, but tonight it felt different, as if it echoed the quiet storm within her. She was almost seven months along now, the reality of her pregnancy settling in with each passing day.

She was excited—so much so that she often found herself daydreaming about her son, wondering what he would look like, how he would sound when he laughed. But beneath the excitement was a layer of fear, a fear she didn't often let herself acknowledge. Would she be enough for him? Could she fill the role of both mother and father, protector and provider?

Her thoughts drifted to Walter, and she felt a pang of frustration. He had promised to be there, to support her and their child, yet his presence had been sporadic at best. She wanted to believe that he could change, that he would step up when it mattered, but experience had taught her to rely on herself.

A sudden knock at the door pulled her from her thoughts, and she stood, her heart racing as she crossed the room. When she opened the door, she was greeted by the warm smile of her brother, Raymond, holding a container of takeout and a bouquet of flowers.

"I thought you could use some company," he said, stepping inside and handing her the flowers.

Tasha smiled, her heart swelling with gratitude. "You're too good to me, Ray."

He chuckled, setting the food on the table. "You're family, Tasha. And family takes care of each other."

They settled at her small kitchen table, unpacking the takeout containers and filling the room with the comforting aroma of hot food. As they ate, Tasha felt a sense of peace, a reminder that she wasn't truly alone. Raymond had been a constant support throughout her pregnancy, and in many ways, he was the one person she could rely on without hesitation.

"So, how are you feeling?" Raymond asked between bites, his gaze warm and attentive.

Tasha hesitated, her thoughts swirling. "Honestly? I'm scared, Ray. I know I can do this, but... sometimes I wonder if it would be easier with Walter here. If he would actually keep his word."

Raymond nodded, his expression thoughtful. "I know it's hard, Tasha. And I wish I could promise you that he'll change. But no matter what he does, you're strong enough to do this on your own. You've got a family who loves you, who's going to be there every step of the way."

Tasha felt tears prick her eyes, and she quickly blinked them away. "Thank you, Ray. I don't know what I'd do without you."

Raymond reached across the table, taking her hand in his. "We're in this together, Tasha. You're not alone, and you never will be."

2

A few days later, Tasha attended a prenatal class at the local community center. She was the only one there without a partner, a fact that hadn't bothered her before, but today, it felt more pronounced. As the instructor guided them through breathing exercises and relaxation techniques, Tasha found herself glancing around, watching as other couples worked together, their hands intertwined, their laughter filling the room.

She closed her eyes, focusing on her own breathing, reminding herself that she was capable, that she didn't need anyone else. But when the class ended and she walked outside, the loneliness hit her like a wave. She had always prided herself on her independence, her ability to handle whatever life threw her way, but right now, she wished for a hand to hold, for someone to share this journey with.

Her phone buzzed with a message, and she pulled it out, seeing a text from Shannon: *Hey, sis! I was thinking we could have a sister night soon—just us, some ice cream, and movies. What do you think?*

Tasha smiled, the timing of the message feeling like an answer to a silent prayer. She quickly typed back, *Yes! I'd love that. When are you free?*

Within minutes, Shannon replied with an enthusiastic, *Tonight! I'll bring the snacks. See you soon.*

Tasha felt a sense of warmth spread through her, a reminder that she didn't have to face this alone. She had her family, her sister, and her faith. And maybe, just maybe, that was enough.

3

Later that evening, Tasha's apartment was filled with laughter and the sweet scent of ice cream and popcorn. She and Shannon lounged on the couch, blankets draped over them as they watched a classic rom-com, laughing at the cheesy dialogue and exaggerated expressions.

As the movie ended, Shannon turned to her, her expression turning serious. "So, how are you really doing, Tasha?"

Tasha sighed, setting her empty ice cream bowl on the coffee table. "Honestly? It's hard, Shan. I feel like I'm on this roller coaster of emotions—one minute I'm excited, the next I'm terrified. And then there's Walter... part of me wants him to be here, but another part of me knows I shouldn't depend on him."

Shannon nodded, reaching over to squeeze her hand. "You're allowed to feel all of that, Tasha. It doesn't make you any less strong. And you don't have to do this alone. We're here for you—for both of you."

Tasha felt a tear slip down her cheek, and she quickly wiped it away. "Thank you, Shan. I don't say it enough, but I'm grateful for you. You and Raymond, you're my rocks."

Shannon smiled, her eyes shining with affection. "We love you, Tasha. And we're going to get through this together. You're not alone, and neither is that little one."

They sat in silence for a moment, the weight of Shannon's words settling over Tasha like a warm embrace. She knew she still had a journey ahead of her, but tonight, she felt a renewed strength—a reminder that she didn't have to carry the weight alone.

4

The following week, Tasha received an unexpected call from Walter. She hesitated before answering, her heart racing as she braced herself for whatever he had to say.

"Hey, Tasha," his voice came through, sounding hesitant, almost apologetic. "I know I haven't been around as much as I should've. But I want to be there for you and the baby. I know I've made mistakes, but I want to make things right."

Tasha took a deep breath, steadying herself. "Walter, I appreciate that, but it's going to take more than words. If you really want to be involved, you have to show up consistently. This isn't just about us—it's about our child."

He was silent for a moment, and then he spoke, his voice filled with determination. "I understand. I'll be there, Tasha. I promise."

After they hung up, Tasha sat in silence, her emotions a mixture of hope and skepticism. She wanted to believe him, wanted to trust that he could change. But she had learned to guard her heart, to rely on herself. She prayed for wisdom, for strength, and for the courage to do what was best for her child, regardless of what Walter chose.

5

The weeks passed, and as Tasha's due date drew closer, she found herself feeling more prepared, more at peace. She had her family by her side, her faith to guide her, and a quiet strength that had grown within her through each challenge.

One evening, as she lay in bed, she whispered a prayer for her son. "Lord, give me the strength to be the mother he needs. Help me to raise him with love, with courage, with faith. And let him always know that he is loved, no matter what."

As she drifted off to sleep, Tasha felt a sense of calm wash over her, a feeling that everything would be okay. She didn't know what the future held, but she knew she was ready to face it with grace, with resilience, and with the unbreakable love of a mother.

Chapter 7: Faith Under Fire

1 Raymond sat at his desk, the church's financial reports spread out in front of him like a battlefield. He had been studying the numbers for hours, yet the path forward remained as unclear as ever. He had done everything in his power to avoid cutting vital programs—programs that had become the heart of Rhema Word Tabernacle's ministry. But the church's budget continued to tighten, and difficult decisions loomed.

A soft knock at his office door broke his concentration, and he looked up to see Deacon Henderson peering inside.

"Got a minute, Pastor?" Henderson asked, stepping in before Raymond could answer.

Raymond managed a weary smile, gesturing for him to sit. "Of course, Deacon. What's on your mind?"

The deacon eased into the chair across from him, his face etched with concern. "Pastor, I know this isn't easy, but we need a plan. The congregation is starting to notice the strain, and some are even beginning to worry about the future of our outreach programs."

Raymond sighed, rubbing a hand over his face. "I know. I don't want to give up on the work we're doing. People depend on us—not just for spiritual guidance, but for real, tangible help."

Henderson nodded thoughtfully. "And I respect that, Pastor. But maybe it's time we take a different approach. Have you thought about reaching out for external support? Perhaps from other churches or local businesses willing to partner with us?"

Raymond considered the suggestion, feeling a flicker of hope. He had always been hesitant to rely on outside help, preferring to keep Rhema Word independent, self-sustained. But as the weight of the crisis pressed down on him, he realized that pride had no place here. His congregation needed him to do whatever it took to keep their doors open, to keep their mission alive.

"Thank you, Deacon," he said, his voice steady. "I'll consider it. And I'll reach out to some of my contacts to see if we can put something together."

Henderson placed a reassuring hand on his shoulder as he stood. "You're not alone in this, Pastor. We're all here to help. And God will see us through, one way or another."

Raymond nodded, grateful for the deacon's support. As the door closed behind Henderson, Raymond leaned back in his chair, a new sense of determination filling his heart. He would not let his congregation down. They had come too far, and he knew he would need every ounce of faith and resilience he possessed to face the challenges ahead.

2

That Sunday, Raymond took to the pulpit with a renewed spirit, his voice strong and filled with conviction as he addressed the congregation.

"Brothers and sisters," he began, his gaze sweeping over the familiar faces in the pews, "we've been blessed to build a community here, a family united by faith, by love, and by a commitment to serve. But as many of you know, we're facing some challenges—challenges that test our resolve, that push us to our limits."

He paused, letting his words sink in, watching as his congregation leaned forward, their expressions filled with empathy and concern.

"I know that some of you have noticed the strain," he continued, his voice softening. "And I want you to know that we're doing everything in our power to keep this church strong, to keep our doors open to those in need. But we can't do it alone. This isn't just a building—it's a family. And as a family, we need to come together, to support one another, to lift each other up."

There was a murmur of agreement, and Raymond felt a surge of gratitude for the loyalty and love that filled his church. He knew that they were willing to stand with him, to fight for the future of Rhema Word. And in that moment, he felt a renewed sense of purpose, a conviction that they would overcome this trial together.

As the service came to a close, members of the congregation approached him, their words of encouragement and promises of support lifting his spirits. Among them was Shannon, standing with Keturah by her side.

"Raymond," she said, her voice warm, "that was a powerful message. You've built something special here."

Raymond felt a pang of emotion as he looked at her, reminded once again of the partnership they had once shared. "Thank you, Shannon. It means a lot to hear that from you."

They shared a moment of silence, both acutely aware of the weight of their past and the unspoken words between them. Finally, Shannon reached out, touching his arm.

"Raymond," she began hesitantly, "if there's anything I can do to help, please let me know. I want to support you, for Keturah's sake—and maybe for ours, too."

Her words took him by surprise, and he felt a flicker of hope, a possibility that perhaps they could rebuild the trust that had once been shattered. "Thank you, Shannon. I'd appreciate that."

As they parted ways, Raymond couldn't shake the feeling that something was shifting, that perhaps God was working in ways he hadn't anticipated.

3

The following week, Raymond arranged a meeting with local business owners and pastors from nearby churches, inviting them to Rhema Word to discuss potential partnerships. He was nervous, aware that seeking help could be seen as a sign of weakness, but he knew that humility was sometimes necessary in the face of adversity.

As the meeting began, he spoke openly about the challenges Rhema Word faced, his voice steady as he laid out his vision for the church's future and his hopes for expanding their outreach. To his relief, many of the attendees responded with enthusiasm, offering financial support, resources, and even volunteers to help keep Rhema Word's programs running.

By the end of the meeting, Raymond felt a sense of relief wash over him. The support of the community had given him the boost he needed, a reminder that they were all united in their mission to serve. As he walked back to his office, he whispered a prayer of gratitude, thanking God for the unexpected blessings that had come his way.

4

That evening, Raymond sat alone in his office, reflecting on the day's events. His thoughts drifted to Shannon once again, and he couldn't shake the feeling that their paths were converging in ways he hadn't foreseen. He thought about Keturah, about the family they had once been, and a part of him wondered if there was still a chance for them to rebuild what had been lost.

With a deep breath, he picked up his phone and sent Shannon a message: *Thank you for your support today. I'd like to talk, if you're open to it. Maybe we can grab coffee sometime?*

To his surprise, her response came almost immediately: *I'd like that. Let's make it happen.*

As he set his phone down, a sense of hope settled over him—a hope that maybe, just maybe, God was leading them back to each other.

5

The next morning, Raymond met Shannon at a quiet coffee shop near her office. They sat across from each other, the weight of their history hanging between them, yet both feeling an unspoken understanding that this was a step toward healing.

"Raymond," Shannon began, her voice steady, "I want you to know that I've been doing a lot of thinking. About us, about our past. And I think it's time I finally let go of the hurt. For Keturah's sake, and for my own."

Raymond nodded, his heart swelling with gratitude. "Shannon, I've made my share of mistakes, and I know I've hurt you. But I've never stopped caring about you, and I want us to find a way to move forward."

They talked for hours, sharing their fears, their regrets, and their hopes for the future. By the time they left the coffee shop, they both felt lighter, as if a burden they had carried for years had finally been lifted.

6

As they stepped outside the coffee shop, Raymond and Shannon paused, both feeling the weight of their conversation settle over them. For years, they had lived in the shadow of their pain, bound by regrets and what-ifs. But today felt different—a beginning rather than an ending.

Shannon wrapped her arms around herself against the brisk morning air. "I didn't realize how much I needed this, Raymond. To finally talk about everything we left unsaid."

Raymond gave her a gentle smile. "Me too. And I want you to know that I'm committed to being there for Keturah, in whatever way you think is best."

Shannon nodded, a soft smile forming on her lips. "I believe you. And I think... I think we owe it to her to try and build something better, even if it's just as friends."

Raymond felt a warmth spread through him at her words. He had hoped for reconciliation, but he knew that friendship could be just as powerful—a foundation built on trust and mutual respect, something that would be strong enough to support them both.

"Thank you, Shannon," he said, his voice filled with sincerity. "I don't take this for granted."

They stood in comfortable silence for a moment before Shannon took a step back, giving him a final nod. "I'll see you at church, then."

Raymond watched her walk away, a sense of peace settling over him. He didn't know what the future held, but for the first time in a long time, he felt ready to face it with an open heart.

7

Later that evening, as Raymond prepared for bed, he reflected on the events of the day, feeling a deep gratitude for the ways God had moved in his life. He knelt beside his bed, bowing his head in prayer.

"Lord, I thank You for the gift of forgiveness, for the chance to rebuild what was broken. I know I've made mistakes, but I ask for Your guidance as I walk this path. Help me to be the father Keturah deserves, the leader my congregation needs, and the man You've called me to be."

As he rose from his prayer, a sense of purpose filled him. He knew that the journey ahead wouldn't be easy, but he was ready to face it with courage and humility, trusting that God's hand would guide him.

For Raymond, this was more than a fresh start. It was a second chance—a chance to rebuild his faith, his family, and his future, one step at a time.

8

Sunday came quickly, and Raymond found himself once again standing at the pulpit, his congregation's eyes fixed on him with an intensity that reminded him of why he had chosen this path. They were his family, each one of them a soul he had been called to shepherd, to guide through both the highs and the lows of life.

As he delivered his sermon, Raymond felt a renewed strength within him, a conviction that extended beyond the words he spoke. He shared his thoughts on resilience, on the power of community, and on the importance of faith in the face of adversity. His voice echoed through the sanctuary, resonating with an energy that came not just from him, but from the faith that filled the room.

After the service, as he greeted members of the congregation, he noticed Shannon standing near the back with Keturah, a quiet smile on her face. He walked over, reaching down to scoop up his daughter, who wrapped her arms around his neck with a delighted giggle.

"Did you like Daddy's sermon?" he asked, smiling as she nodded enthusiastically.

"It was the best one yet!" she exclaimed, her eyes sparkling with joy.

Raymond looked at Shannon, a soft gratitude in his gaze. "Thank you for bringing her today."

Shannon nodded, her smile warm. "She wanted to see you, and... I think I needed to be here too."

They shared a quiet moment, each understanding the significance of this new beginning. There was still healing to be done, but they were moving forward, united by a common love for their daughter and a shared commitment to the future.

9

As the weeks passed, Raymond continued to pour himself into his work, his family, and his faith. The partnerships he had formed with local businesses and churches began to bear fruit, bringing in the resources Rhema Word needed to sustain its programs. His congregation grew stronger, bound by a renewed sense of unity and purpose.

His relationship with Shannon also grew, albeit slowly and cautiously. They began to meet regularly with Keturah, attending her school events and spending time together as a family. Their bond deepened, not in the way it once had, but in a way that felt honest, rooted in forgiveness and mutual respect.

One evening, after a long day at the church, Raymond sat in his office, reflecting on the journey that had brought him here. He thought about the challenges he had faced, the mistakes he had made, and the grace he had received. He knew that he was far from perfect, but he was grateful for the lessons he had learned, the faith that had carried him through, and the love that had been restored in his life.

He picked up his Bible, flipping through the familiar pages until he found the passage he was searching for. *"And we know that all things work together for good to those who love God, to those who are called according to His purpose."* The words resonated within him, a reminder that even in the darkest moments, God's hand was at work, weaving together a tapestry of redemption, of healing, of grace.

As he closed his Bible, Raymond felt a sense of peace wash over him, a quiet assurance that he was exactly where he was meant to be. And as he looked out at the city lights beyond his window, he whispered a prayer of gratitude, his heart full, his spirit renewed.

Chapter 8: Crossroads of the Heart

1 Shannon lingered at the entrance of her apartment, her fingers tracing the key in her hand as she replayed the evening with Raymond and Keturah in her mind. They had gone to the zoo as a family, wandering through exhibits and laughing at Keturah's excitement over the animals. Raymond had been in his element, his warmth and attentiveness drawing Shannon in despite the guarded part of her heart.

She had felt a quiet joy, watching her daughter's face light up and seeing the way Raymond looked at her—as if they were a family again, if only for the afternoon. But now, back in the solitude of her home, the familiar doubts crept in. Was she ready to open her heart to Raymond again? Did she even want that?

The truth was, while Raymond seemed to view their outings as steps toward reconciliation, Shannon wasn't so sure. She enjoyed the moments they shared, but there was a lingering hesitation she couldn't ignore. Perhaps that was why she kept seeing Robert.

She hadn't told Raymond about Robert, and guilt gnawed at her for keeping it from him. Yet, her connection with Robert felt different—easy, uncomplicated by the baggage she and Raymond carried. It was refreshing, but it also left her feeling torn, caught between the past and the possibility of a future that didn't include Raymond.

Shannon took a deep breath, stepping inside and closing the door behind her. She knew she needed to sort out her feelings, but the answers remained elusive, hidden behind layers of hurt and hope.

2

The next day, Shannon met Robert for lunch at a restaurant near her office. He greeted her with his usual smile, warm and confident, and Shannon felt a sense of comfort in his presence. They had fallen into a steady rhythm over the past few weeks, sharing stories about work, life, and everything in between. And though she hadn't shared much about her past with Raymond, Robert seemed to understand her need for space, for patience.

"You look distracted," he observed, studying her with genuine concern. "Something on your mind?"

Shannon hesitated, the familiar conflict rising within her. "I've just been spending a lot of time with my daughter and... and her father, trying to give Keturah a sense of family."

Robert nodded, his expression understanding. "It makes sense. She deserves that, and so do you."

His words struck a chord, bringing a rush of mixed emotions. She knew she deserved happiness, stability—but she wasn't sure if that was with Raymond or if it could be with someone new. She felt a pang of guilt for keeping Robert in the dark, yet the uncertainty kept her from fully opening up.

Robert reached across the table, his hand covering hers in a gesture of reassurance. "I like spending time with you, Shannon. And I hope, wherever this goes, that we're moving toward something real. But only if you're ready."

Shannon managed a small smile, appreciating his honesty and patience. "I'm working through a lot right now. But I do want to be here with you."

Robert returned her smile, squeezing her hand. "Take all the time you need. I'm not going anywhere."

For a brief moment, Shannon felt the weight lift, soothed by Robert's understanding. Yet as they left the restaurant, she knew the questions within her remained, waiting for answers she wasn't sure she was ready to face.

3

That weekend, Shannon met Raymond and Keturah at the park for a picnic. It was something they had started doing as a way to reconnect, to give Keturah a sense of family, and while Shannon enjoyed these outings, her heart remained divided.

As they spread out the picnic blanket and Keturah began setting up her toys, Raymond turned to Shannon with a quiet smile. "I'm glad we're doing this. It feels good, doesn't it?"

Shannon returned his smile, though she felt a pang of guilt. "It does. I think it's good for Keturah to see us together."

Raymond nodded, but his gaze lingered on her, a hint of something deeper in his eyes. "Maybe it's good for us, too. I've missed this, Shannon. I've missed us."

Her heart tightened at his words, torn between the warmth of his sincerity and the doubts that had been growing within her. She looked away, her gaze drifting to Keturah as she played, feeling the weight of the unspoken words between them.

She hadn't told Raymond about Robert, hadn't shared the fact that she was exploring the possibility of moving on. Part of her worried it would hurt him, but another part feared it would shatter whatever fragile connection they were rebuilding. Yet, keeping it from him felt like a betrayal—a betrayal of the trust they were slowly trying to restore.

As the afternoon wore on, Shannon found herself withdrawing, her mind preoccupied with the choices before her. When they said their goodbyes, she hugged Keturah tightly, feeling the familiar ache in her chest as she watched Raymond and their daughter walk away.

4

That evening, Shannon sat in her living room, her thoughts a tangled mess of emotions. She knew she couldn't keep going like this, torn between two worlds, unable to fully commit to either. If she wanted to move forward, she had to confront her feelings, to make a decision—one that would either open the door to reconciliation with Raymond or allow her to explore something new with Robert.

Taking a deep breath, she picked up her phone and called her sister, Tasha. Tasha answered on the second ring, her voice bright and cheerful. "Hey, Shan! What's up?"

"I need advice," Shannon admitted, her voice hesitant. "About Raymond, about Robert... about everything."

There was a pause, and then Tasha's voice softened. "I'm here, sis. Talk to me."

Shannon explained her situation, sharing the doubts and fears she had been carrying, the conflict between the comfort of her past and the excitement of something new. Tasha listened patiently, offering a few words of encouragement but mostly letting Shannon pour out her heart.

"Shannon," Tasha said finally, her tone thoughtful, "I know you want to make the right choice, but there's no clear answer here. You have to trust what feels right, not just for you, but for Keturah. And maybe that means being honest with Raymond about Robert."

Shannon felt a knot of anxiety tighten in her chest. "I know. I just... I don't want to hurt him, Tasha. But I also don't want to keep hiding this. It's not fair to anyone."

"Then maybe it's time to tell him," Tasha suggested gently. "If you're serious about moving on, he deserves to know. But if there's still something there, if you're not ready to let go of him, then maybe that's worth exploring too."

Shannon sighed, the weight of her decision pressing down on her. "I just wish it was easier."

Tasha chuckled softly. "Love isn't easy, Shannon. But if you follow your heart, you'll make the right choice."

After they hung up, Shannon sat in silence, Tasha's words echoing in her mind. She knew what she had to do, even if it meant risking the fragile peace she and Raymond had built.

5

The following day, Shannon met Raymond for coffee. They sat across from each other in a quiet corner of the cafe, the familiarity of the moment bringing a pang of nostalgia.

"Thank you for meeting me," Shannon began, her hands twisting nervously in her lap. "There's something I need to tell you."

Raymond looked at her, his expression open and attentive. "Of course. What's on your mind?"

Shannon took a deep breath, steadying herself. "Raymond, I've been seeing someone... someone from work. His name is Robert."

She watched as a flicker of surprise crossed his face, followed by a look of quiet disappointment. He nodded slowly, processing her words. "I see."

"It's still new," she added quickly, feeling a need to soften the impact. "But I wanted to be honest with you. I didn't want you to find out from anyone else."

Raymond's gaze held hers, his voice calm but filled with emotion. "Thank you for telling me, Shannon. I appreciate the honesty. I just... I thought maybe we were moving toward something ourselves."

Shannon's heart ached at his words, the vulnerability in his eyes. "Raymond, I care about you. I always will. But... I don't know if we can ever go back to what we had. There's so much history, so much pain. And while I want to give Keturah a sense of family, I also want to be true to myself."

He nodded, his expression resigned but understanding. "I want you to be happy, Shannon. Whether that's with me or someone else."

They sat in silence, the weight of her confession settling between them. Shannon felt a mixture of relief and sadness, knowing she had done the right thing but feeling the loss of a dream she hadn't fully let go of.

As they left the cafe, Shannon felt a sense of closure, a quiet acceptance of the path she had chosen. And as she walked away, she whispered a silent prayer for guidance, trusting that, wherever life led her, she would find peace.

6

Days passed, and the weight of her conversation with Raymond lingered in Shannon's heart. Though she had been honest with him, the guilt and uncertainty still gnawed at her. She tried to focus on work, but even the familiar rhythm of her career couldn't drown out her conflicted emotions.

One evening, after a particularly draining board meeting, Shannon found herself standing by the floor-to-ceiling windows of her office, staring out at the shimmering city lights. The skyline stretched endlessly, full of possibilities—yet she felt trapped, caught in the web of her choices.

Her phone buzzed, pulling her from her thoughts. It was a text from Robert:

Robert: *Thinking of you. Hope you're okay.*

Her chest tightened at his simple, thoughtful words. Despite her confusion about Raymond, she couldn't deny how safe and seen Robert made her feel. He didn't pressure her or demand answers she couldn't give. He just... showed up.

Before she could overthink it, she replied:

Shannon: *I could use some company... are you free?*

His response came almost instantly.

Robert: *Always.*

7

Later that evening, Robert arrived at Shannon's apartment, carrying a small bag of takeout from her favorite Thai restaurant. The comforting scent of basil and spices filled the room as they settled on the couch, the soft hum of jazz playing in the background.

"Rough day?" he asked gently, handing her a plate.

She nodded, sighing as she took a bite of the savory noodles. "Just... a lot on my mind."

Robert watched her carefully, his expression both curious and patient. "You don't have to explain. I'm here."

His quiet understanding was like a balm to her weary soul. She placed her plate on the coffee table and leaned back, resting her head on the couch. "Thank you... for being so patient with me."

He reached for her hand, threading his fingers through hers. "You're worth the wait."

His words sent a wave of warmth through her, melting some of the ice she had been holding onto for so long. In that moment, she allowed herself to be fully present, to let down her guard—just a little.

8

But even in the comfort of Robert's presence, Shannon couldn't shake the memory of Raymond's face when she told him about their relationship. His expression, filled with quiet acceptance but undeniable hurt, haunted her.

A few nights later, she found herself sitting alone in her living room, the soft glow of the fireplace casting flickering shadows across the walls. She cradled a cup of tea in her hands, seeking warmth that couldn't quite reach her heart.

Her journal lay open on the coffee table, its pages inviting her to spill the thoughts she couldn't voice aloud. After a moment's hesitation, she picked up her pen:

"Lord... I don't know where this road leads. I thought being honest would make things clearer, but it only seems to have complicated everything. I care about Robert... but a part of me still feels tied to Raymond. Please... guide my steps."

Her hand trembled as she set the pen down, emotions swirling in a confusing storm of love, regret, and hope.

9

That weekend, Shannon took Keturah to a community art fair—a tradition they had shared for years. Keturah loved painting and crafts, and Shannon cherished the moments when her daughter's creativity sparkled with pure joy.

"Mommy, look!" Keturah tugged her hand excitedly, pulling her toward a booth filled with hand-painted ceramic mugs. "Can we make one together?"

Shannon smiled, her heart swelling with affection. "Of course, baby."

They sat at the art station, Keturah chattering happily as she painted her mug with bright, swirling colors. Shannon's own brush moved slowly, her mind drifting to the complexities of her heart.

"Are you sad, Mommy?" Keturah's soft voice broke through her thoughts.

Shannon blinked, surprised by the question. "Why would you think that, sweetheart?"

Keturah shrugged, her small hands still gripping the paintbrush. "You look sad sometimes… like you're thinking about something really hard."

Emotion tightened in Shannon's throat, but she managed a smile. "I'm okay, baby. Sometimes grown-ups have a lot on their minds. But being here with you makes me really happy."

Satisfied with the answer, Keturah beamed and went back to painting. Shannon watched her daughter with a mixture of pride and longing, realizing how much she wanted to set a better example—for herself and for Keturah.

She needed to stop living in the past and start embracing the life still waiting in front of her.

10

That night, Shannon tucked Keturah into bed, lingering a moment longer than usual. As she kissed her daughter's forehead, she whispered, "I love you more than anything."

Keturah snuggled into her blankets, her voice drowsy but certain. "I love you too, Mommy."

As Shannon turned off the light and closed the door, she felt a quiet sense of clarity she hadn't experienced in months. For the first time, she allowed herself to believe that she could find peace—not by erasing the past, but by accepting it.

Taking a deep breath, she picked up her phone and sent a message she had been holding back for too long:

Shannon: *Hey Robert... I think I'm ready to talk about where this is going.*

Chapter 9: Strength Renewed

1 Tasha walked through the aisles of the baby store, her hand resting on her belly as she scanned the shelves. Her due date was only a few weeks away, and while she had most of the essentials, there were still a few last-minute items she needed. But as she moved from aisle to aisle, she felt an unease growing within her—a mixture of excitement and anxiety as the reality of motherhood set in.

She paused in front of a display of tiny onesies, imagining her son's face, his smile, his little fingers curling around hers. It was a comforting thought, yet it also filled her with an overwhelming sense of responsibility. Would she be enough for him? Could she give him the love and stability he deserved, even without a partner by her side?

Her thoughts were interrupted by the buzzing of her phone. She glanced at the screen and saw a message from Walter: *Can we talk?*

She stared at the words, feeling a familiar tension settle in her chest. Walter had been reaching out more frequently over the past few weeks, claiming he wanted to be involved, that he was ready to step up. But his promises were still just words to her, and she couldn't afford to build her hopes on empty assurances.

Taking a deep breath, she typed back a simple response: *Meet me at the park in an hour.*

2

An hour later, Tasha sat on a bench at the park, watching as children ran across the grass, their laughter filling the air. She placed a protective hand on her belly, feeling the gentle kicks of her son as she waited for Walter to arrive.

When he finally appeared, she could see the uncertainty in his eyes as he approached her. He looked different—tired, almost humbled. But Tasha had learned to guard her heart, to approach his words with caution.

"Tasha," he began, sitting down beside her, "thank you for meeting with me."

She nodded, keeping her expression neutral. "What did you want to talk about, Walter?"

He sighed, running a hand through his hair. "I know I haven't been there for you, or for our son, the way I should have been. And I know I've made a lot of mistakes. But I want to be a part of his life. I want to be a father to him."

Tasha looked at him, her heart conflicted. She wanted to believe him, to trust that he could change, but the scars of his past behavior lingered, a reminder of the pain he had caused.

"Walter," she said softly, her voice steady, "it's going to take more than words. I need consistency, reliability. I can't afford to have someone who's in and out of his life, who only shows up when it's convenient."

He nodded, his gaze dropping to the ground. "I understand. And I'm willing to prove myself, Tasha. I don't expect you to trust me right away, but I want to earn it."

For a moment, Tasha allowed herself to hope, to imagine a future where Walter was a steady presence for their son. But she knew that actions spoke louder than promises, and she couldn't allow herself to be swayed by his words alone.

"Then show me," she replied, her tone firm but not unkind. "Be there. Show up. And maybe, in time, I'll be able to trust you again."

They sat in silence for a few moments, the weight of her words settling between them. Tasha felt a mixture of relief and caution, knowing she had set clear boundaries, but also knowing that only time would reveal whether he would follow through.

3

As Tasha walked back to her apartment, she felt a strange mixture of exhaustion and empowerment. She had faced Walter, set her expectations, and reclaimed control over her future. Yet, the uncertainty still lingered—a reminder of the unpredictability of life, especially as a single mother.

When she reached her apartment, she found her mother, Katherine, waiting for her, a gentle smile on her face.

"How's my girl doing?" Katherine asked, her eyes filled with warmth as she placed a hand on Tasha's shoulder.

Tasha managed a small smile. "Tired, Mama. And nervous. I met with Walter today."

Katherine raised an eyebrow, her expression sympathetic. "And how did that go?"

Tasha sighed, sinking onto the couch. "He says he wants to be involved, that he wants to be there for our son. But I've heard it all before. I don't know if I can believe him."

Katherine sat beside her, wrapping an arm around her shoulders. "You have every right to protect your heart, Tasha. And your son's. But remember, people can change. Sometimes it takes a while, and sometimes they don't get it right on the first try."

Tasha leaned into her mother's embrace, feeling a sense of comfort in her presence. "I just don't want to get my hopes up. I don't want to build a future around promises that might never come true."

Her mother nodded, her voice gentle. "Then keep doing what you're doing, honey. Build a life for you and your son that doesn't rely on anyone else. If Walter wants to be part of that, let him earn it. And if not, you're strong enough to do this on your own."

Tasha felt tears prick her eyes, grateful for her mother's unwavering support. She knew she had a long road ahead of her, but with her family by her side, she felt a renewed sense of courage, a belief that she could face whatever came her way.

4

As the weeks passed, Tasha threw herself into preparing for her son's arrival. She spent her days arranging the nursery, organizing baby clothes, and attending prenatal classes. Raymond and Shannon visited often, helping with last-minute preparations and offering words of encouragement. Their support reminded her of the strength in family, a foundation that would carry her through this journey.

One evening, as she sat in the nursery folding baby clothes, Shannon joined her, settling into the chair across from her with a warm smile.

"You're going to be an amazing mom, Tasha," Shannon said, her tone filled with admiration. "Your son is so lucky to have you."

Tasha looked at her sister, feeling a swell of gratitude. "Thank you, Shan. I just... I want to give him the best life possible, you know? I want him to feel loved, no matter what."

Shannon reached over, squeezing her hand. "And he will. Because he has you, and he has all of us. He's already so loved, Tasha. You're not alone in this."

Tasha nodded, feeling a warmth spread through her heart. She knew that no matter what happened with Walter, she had a family who would support her, who would stand by her and her son. And that knowledge brought her a sense of peace, a belief that she could face the challenges of motherhood with courage and grace.

5

The night before her due date, Tasha lay in bed, her mind racing with a mixture of excitement and nervous anticipation. She knew that everything was about to change, that her life would be forever transformed by the arrival of her son. And while she still had fears, still had doubts, she also felt a deep sense of purpose—a calling that had grown within her as her child grew inside her.

In the quiet of the night, she whispered a prayer, her voice filled with emotion. "Lord, give me the strength to be the mother he deserves. Help me to guide him, to love him, to teach him the values that will carry him through life. And let him always know that he is loved, that he is cherished, even in the hardest of times."

As she closed her eyes, a sense of calm washed over her, a feeling that everything would be okay. She didn't know what the future held, but she knew she was ready to face it with faith, with resilience, and with the unbreakable love of a mother.

And as sleep claimed her, she felt the gentle reassurance that she was exactly where she was meant to be—a mother, a daughter, a sister, and a woman standing strong in the face of life's uncertainties.

Chapter 10: A Heart in Transition

1 Raymond sat alone in his office at Rhema Word Tabernacle, his gaze unfocused as he replayed his recent conversation with Shannon. The news that she was seeing someone else had been a blow he hadn't seen coming. He'd allowed himself to hope that the time they had been spending together as a family was leading to something more—a chance to rebuild what had once been broken. But now, that hope felt as fragile as dust, slipping through his fingers.

He ran a hand over his face, leaning back in his chair. He wanted to be happy for Shannon, to support her in her choices, especially if they made her happy. Yet, part of him couldn't let go of the dream he'd held onto—that one day, they might find their way back to each other.

"Lord," he whispered, his voice barely audible, "give me the strength to let her go if that's Your will. Help me to trust Your plan, even if it's not the one I wanted."

2

The following Sunday, Raymond stood at the pulpit, facing his congregation with a heart that felt both heavy and hopeful. His sermon was on the theme of surrender—of giving one's desires and plans to God, trusting that He knew what was best.

"We all have dreams, goals, things we want to achieve," he said, his voice steady yet laced with emotion. "But sometimes, God calls us to let go, to trust that He knows what we need better than we do. And when we surrender, we open the door for healing, for growth, for the unexpected blessings that come from a heart that is truly yielded to Him."

He could see his words resonating with the congregation, their faces reflecting the struggles they, too, carried. And in that moment, Raymond felt a sense of peace, a quiet assurance that maybe, just maybe, he was exactly where he was meant to be. As he closed the service, he whispered a silent prayer, asking for the courage to walk this path, even if it meant letting go of the love he had held onto for so long.

3

Later that evening, Raymond sat at home, scrolling through old photos on his phone. He paused on a picture of him and Shannon, taken years ago on a warm summer day. They were both laughing, Keturah held between them, her tiny face alight with joy. The image brought a bittersweet ache to his heart, a reminder of the life they had built and the dreams that had once felt so certain.

A knock at the door interrupted his thoughts, and he stood, surprised to see Deacon Henderson waiting outside, a thoughtful look on his face.

"Evening, Pastor," Henderson greeted him, stepping inside. "Hope I'm not interrupting."

Raymond managed a smile. "Not at all, Deacon. What's on your mind?"

Henderson settled onto the couch, his expression serious. "I noticed you seemed... a bit off today during the service. I know it's none of my business, but you've been carrying a lot lately, and I wanted to make sure you're alright."

Raymond sighed, grateful for the concern. "Thank you, Deacon. It's just... personal matters. I'm working through some things, trying to let go of what I thought my future would look like."

Henderson nodded, his gaze compassionate. "I understand, Pastor. But remember, sometimes God has a way of taking our plans and transforming them into something better than we could have imagined. Trust in His timing, and don't be afraid to lean on your family here at Rhema Word. We're all here for you."

Raymond felt a surge of gratitude, the words a balm to his weary spirit. "Thank you, Deacon. I needed to hear that."

As Henderson left, Raymond felt a renewed sense of purpose, a reminder that he wasn't alone in this journey. He had a congregation, a community that cared for him, and perhaps it was time to shift his focus from what he had lost to the blessings that still surrounded him.

4

Over the next few weeks, Raymond poured himself into his work, focusing on his responsibilities as a pastor, a father, and a leader. He began to find comfort in the routines of his ministry, the joy of serving others, and the sense of purpose that came from helping his congregation grow in faith.

One afternoon, he received a call from Shannon. Her voice was warm, and though he still felt a pang of longing when he heard it, he reminded himself of the path he was on—a path of release, of trust, of surrender.

"Raymond," she began, her tone gentle, "I just wanted to thank you for everything you've done for Keturah and me. I know things haven't been easy, but I appreciate how supportive you've been."

Raymond felt a mixture of pride and sadness, knowing that he would always care for her, even if they weren't meant to be together. "You don't have to thank me, Shannon. Keturah and you will always be a part of my life. I'm grateful for the time we share, even if it's not the way I once imagined."

There was a pause, and then she spoke again, her voice soft. "I just want you to know that I'll always value our family, Raymond. No matter what happens."

As they ended the call, Raymond felt a sense of closure, a quiet acceptance that allowed him to release some of the hurt, some of the longing. He knew that the future was uncertain, but he was ready to face it with faith and an open heart.

5

One evening, Raymond met with a few of his close friends from seminary who were in town visiting. They spent hours reminiscing, sharing stories, and talking about their ministries, each of them reflecting on the twists and turns their lives had taken since their early days.

One of his friends, Pastor David, noticed Raymond's contemplative mood and pulled him aside. "You seem different, Ray. Like you're carrying something heavy."

Raymond hesitated, then nodded. "I am. I thought I had a second chance with Shannon, that we could rebuild what was broken. But she's moved on, and now I'm trying to figure out where I go from here."

David placed a reassuring hand on his shoulder. "You know, sometimes letting go is the only way we can truly grow. If Shannon's path is leading her in a different direction, maybe that's God's way of telling you that there's something else waiting for you—something that's meant just for you."

Raymond listened, feeling the wisdom in his friend's words resonate within him. It was time to let go of what he had envisioned and embrace whatever God had in store for him. He didn't know what that would look like, but he was ready to step forward in faith, trusting that his heart would heal and that new doors would open.

6

As Raymond returned to his routine, he began to feel a shift in his spirit, a sense of peace that grew with each day. He continued spending time with Keturah, cherishing every moment with her, knowing that he could still be a source of strength and love in her life. And in his ministry, he found a renewed passion, a calling that filled the spaces in his heart where hurt had once lingered.

One Sunday morning, as he stood at the pulpit, Raymond looked out over his congregation, feeling a deep gratitude for the people he had been called to serve. He spoke about resilience, about finding hope in unexpected places, about the strength that came from surrender.

"In life, we don't always get what we want," he said, his voice steady. "But when we trust in God's plan, we find that He often gives us what we need. And sometimes, the greatest blessings come not from what we hold onto, but from what we're willing to let go."

As he closed the service, he felt a sense of release, a quiet joy that filled him with hope. He didn't know what the future held, but he was ready to embrace it with faith, with gratitude, and with an open heart.

Chapter 11: Matters of the Heart

1 Shannon sat in her office, staring at the glowing screen of her laptop, but her mind was far from the presentation she was supposed to be preparing. The last few weeks had been a whirlwind of emotions—navigating her growing relationship with Robert, the time she spent with Raymond and Keturah, and the quiet moments at night when she felt caught between two worlds.

Robert had been nothing but kind and attentive, making her feel valued in ways she hadn't experienced in a long time. Yet, every time she saw Raymond, she couldn't help but feel a tug at her heart, a lingering connection that refused to fade.

Her phone buzzed on the desk, pulling her from her thoughts. It was a message from Raymond: *Keturah has a school play next Friday. Want to go together?*

Shannon sighed, her heart tightening. She appreciated the way Raymond was stepping up as a father, making Keturah a priority in ways he hadn't during their marriage. But his continued effort to include her in family moments left her feeling conflicted, unsure of where the boundaries should lie.

She typed a quick response: *Yes, let's plan on it. Keturah will be excited.*

After hitting send, she leaned back in her chair, staring at the ceiling. She knew she needed to figure out her feelings—what she wanted, who she wanted—and soon. Otherwise, she risked hurting not only herself but the people she cared about most.

2

That evening, Shannon met Robert for dinner at an upscale restaurant downtown. He had made reservations at her favorite spot, a thoughtful gesture that reminded her why she had been drawn to him in the first place. As they sat across from each other, sharing stories about their day, Shannon found herself smiling, feeling the warmth of his presence.

"You've been quiet lately," Robert said, studying her with a gentle expression. "Is everything okay?"

Shannon hesitated, swirling the wine in her glass. "I've just been... thinking a lot. About Keturah, about my family. It's a lot to juggle sometimes."

Robert reached across the table, covering her hand with his. "I get it. And I don't want to add to your stress, Shannon. I just want to be here for you, however you need me."

His words were sincere, and Shannon felt a pang of guilt for the doubts she carried. She wanted to fully embrace this new chapter with Robert, to leave the past behind. But every time she tried, her heart pulled her back to Raymond.

"Thank you," she said softly, offering him a small smile. "That means a lot to me."

As the evening went on, Shannon felt herself relax, enjoying the ease of their conversation. But even as she laughed at Robert's jokes and appreciated his kindness, a part of her couldn't help but wonder if she was truly ready to move on—or if she was simply trying to convince herself she was.

3

The night of Keturah's school play arrived, and Shannon found herself sitting beside Raymond in the crowded auditorium. They had arrived early to save good seats, and now they sat together, flipping through the program as they waited for the performance to begin.

Keturah had been thrilled to hear they would both be there, her excitement spilling over during the ride to school that morning. "I'm so happy you and Daddy are coming together!" she had exclaimed, her smile wide.

Shannon had felt a pang of guilt at her daughter's words, knowing that Keturah still harbored hope for something more. And as she sat beside Raymond now, she couldn't help but feel the weight of those expectations.

"You seem distracted," Raymond said, his voice quiet enough not to draw attention.

Shannon glanced at him, offering a quick smile. "Just thinking about how excited Keturah is for tonight. She's been practicing her lines non-stop."

Raymond chuckled, his expression softening. "She's been talking about it all week. I'm proud of her."

As the lights dimmed and the play began, Shannon found herself watching Raymond out of the corner of her eye. He was fully engaged, his focus entirely on Keturah, and she felt a swell of admiration for the father he was becoming. It was a side of him she hadn't always seen during their marriage, and it made her question whether she had been too quick to let go—or if they had simply needed time to grow.

4

After the play, the three of them went out for ice cream, Keturah chattering excitedly about her performance while Shannon and Raymond listened with smiles. It felt like old times, the kind of family outing they used to have before everything fell apart. But as much as Shannon cherished the moment, she couldn't ignore the voice in her head reminding her that things were different now.

Later that night, after putting Keturah to bed, Shannon sat alone in her living room, replaying the evening in her mind. She thought about the way Raymond had smiled at her, the way his presence felt so familiar, so comfortable. And then she thought about Robert—the warmth of his attention, the way he made her feel seen.

She was caught between two worlds, two men, and two versions of what her life could be. One was rooted in the past, a love that had weathered storms but left scars. The other was new, fresh, and unburdened by history.

Taking a deep breath, Shannon picked up her phone and dialed Tasha's number. Her sister answered on the second ring, her voice bright despite the late hour.

"Hey, Shan! What's up?"

"I need your advice," Shannon admitted, her voice trembling slightly. "I'm so confused, Tasha. I feel like I'm being pulled in two directions, and I don't know what to do."

Tasha was silent for a moment before responding, her tone gentle. "You're talking about Raymond and Robert, aren't you?"

Shannon nodded, even though her sister couldn't see her. "I don't want to hurt anyone, Tasha. But I don't know where my heart is."

Tasha's voice was calm and steady. "Shannon, only you can decide what's right for you. But whatever you choose, make sure it's what makes you happy—not what you think you're supposed to do or what anyone else expects."

Shannon felt tears prick her eyes, grateful for her sister's wisdom. "Thank you, Tasha. I just... I wish it was easier."

"Love's never easy," Tasha replied with a soft laugh. "But it's worth it when it's real. Trust your heart, Shannon. It won't lead you wrong."

5

The following morning, Shannon woke with a sense of clarity she hadn't felt in weeks. She didn't have all the answers, but she knew it was time to start being honest—with herself, with Robert, and with Raymond. It wouldn't be easy, but she owed it to all of them to face the truth.

As she sipped her coffee, watching the sun rise over the city, she whispered a quiet prayer. "Lord, guide me. Help me make the right choice, not just for me, but for Keturah. Give me the courage to follow my heart, wherever it leads."

And as the day began, Shannon felt a sense of peace settle over her, a quiet assurance that she was ready to take the next step—whatever that might be.

Chapter 12: A New Chapter

1 Raymond stood at the entrance of the community center, reviewing his notes for the leadership workshop he had agreed to host. It was a small event organized by a local non-profit, and though his schedule was packed, he had been drawn to the opportunity to connect with others outside his congregation.

As attendees trickled in, Raymond greeted them warmly, shaking hands and exchanging introductions. He was mid-conversation with a local entrepreneur when a voice behind him caught his attention.

"Pastor Raymond Johnson?"

He turned to see a woman approaching, her smile warm and confident. She was striking—not in an ostentatious way, but with a quiet elegance that immediately put him at ease. She extended her hand, her grip firm yet gentle.

"Hi, I'm Vanessa Carter," she said. "I work with Empower Her, the women's advocacy group partnering with this event. Thank you for volunteering your time."

Raymond returned her smile, feeling an unexpected sense of familiarity. "It's my pleasure. I've heard great things about the work you're doing."

Vanessa nodded, her expression brightening. "We're passionate about building stronger communities, and it's leaders like you who help make that possible."

Their exchange was brief, interrupted by the start of the workshop, but something about Vanessa lingered in Raymond's mind as the session began. She exuded a calm confidence, a presence that was both inspiring and comforting.

2

As the workshop ended, Raymond stayed behind to help pack up the materials, chatting with attendees as they left. Vanessa remained as well, assisting her team and occasionally glancing in his direction.

When the room was nearly empty, she approached him again, her smile easy and genuine. "You're a natural up there," she said, motioning to the now-vacant podium. "The way you connected with everyone—it's not something you see every day."

Raymond chuckled, shaking his head. "It's just years of practice. Being a pastor means learning to speak to people where they are."

"Well, it shows," Vanessa replied, her tone sincere. "You made some of those folks feel seen today, and that's a gift."

For a moment, they stood in a comfortable silence, the energy in the room still buzzing from the success of the event. Raymond felt an unusual ease in her presence, a feeling he hadn't experienced in a long time.

"So, Vanessa," he said, breaking the silence, "how did you get involved with Empower Her?"

She leaned against the table, her expression softening. "I used to work in corporate marketing, but I felt like something was missing. I wanted to do something that mattered, something that made a real difference. So, a few years ago, I left that world behind and started working with non-profits. It's been the most rewarding decision of my life."

Raymond nodded, impressed by her conviction. "That's a big leap of faith."

"It was," she admitted, her gaze meeting his. "But sometimes, the best things in life require a little risk."

Her words struck a chord, and Raymond found himself wondering if this chance encounter might be one of those moments—a nudge toward something new, something unexpected.

3

Over the next few weeks, Raymond and Vanessa crossed paths several times, each interaction deepening their connection. She began attending services at Rhema Word, quietly sitting in the back pew and listening intently to his sermons. Afterward, they would often talk—about faith, about community, about their shared passion for helping others.

It wasn't long before members of the congregation began to notice the subtle shift in Raymond's demeanor. He seemed lighter, more at ease, and though he hadn't spoken openly about his growing friendship with Vanessa, it was clear that she had brought something new into his life.

One afternoon, as they sat together in a quiet corner of a coffee shop, Vanessa looked at him with a thoughtful expression. "Raymond, I know you're still healing from your past, but I want you to know that I'm here—no expectations, no pressure. Just... here."

Her honesty caught him off guard, and for a moment, he didn't know how to respond. He had spent so much time focused on his responsibilities, on his daughter, on his congregation, that he hadn't allowed himself to consider the possibility of opening his heart again.

"Thank you, Vanessa," he said finally, his voice soft. "That means more than you know."

4

That evening, Raymond found himself reflecting on the past few months—the steps he had taken toward healing, the unexpected ways God had worked in his life. He thought about Shannon, about the love they had shared and the ways they had grown apart. And now, he thought about Vanessa, the quiet strength she brought, the sense of possibility she represented.

As he knelt to pray, he asked for clarity, for wisdom, for the courage to move forward without fear. "Lord," he whispered, "thank You for the people You've placed in my life, for the lessons You've taught me through pain and through joy. Help me to follow Your lead, wherever it may take me."

5

The next Sunday, Vanessa arrived at Rhema Word with a group of women from Empower Her. Raymond greeted them warmly, feeling a sense of pride as he introduced her to members of the congregation. He couldn't help but notice the way she fit seamlessly into the community, her warmth and authenticity drawing people in.

As the service began, Raymond felt a sense of peace settle over him. He didn't know what the future held, but he knew he was ready to embrace it with faith and an open heart. Whether his journey with Vanessa led to something more or remained a friendship, he trusted that it was part of God's plan.

And as he looked out over the congregation, his gaze lingering on Vanessa for just a moment, he felt a quiet hope blooming within him—a hope that, even in the midst of uncertainty, new beginnings were always possible.

6

The week after Vanessa's first Sunday at Rhema Word, Raymond found himself looking forward to seeing her again—not just at church but beyond its walls. Their conversations had awakened something he thought he'd buried—hope, companionship, and the possibility of sharing his life with someone new.

One quiet afternoon, he decided to visit the community center where Empower Her held weekly outreach programs. He hadn't told Vanessa he was coming, wanting to surprise her while offering support. As he entered the bustling center, he saw her at the front of the room, speaking passionately to a group of young women about personal development and leadership.

"...You are capable of greatness," Vanessa urged, her voice steady and encouraging. "Your past doesn't define your future—only you can do that."

Raymond lingered near the doorway, watching her with quiet admiration. She was magnetic, her sincerity radiating with every word she spoke. When she noticed him, her eyes widened in surprise but quickly softened into a warm smile.

As the session ended, she approached him, still glowing with energy from the event. "You didn't tell me you were coming," she teased.

"I wanted to see what you're building here," he replied, his voice sincere. "It's incredible, Vanessa. You're incredible."

Her expression softened further, a hint of vulnerability shining through. "Thank you, Raymond. That means a lot."

They stood in comfortable silence until Vanessa gestured toward the now-empty room. "We're about to pack up. Want to lend a hand?"

"With pleasure," he answered, rolling up his sleeves.

7

After packing up, Raymond and Vanessa strolled along the nearby park trail, the crisp autumn air wrapping around them. The late afternoon sun cast a golden glow over the trees, creating a serene backdrop for their conversation.

"I never asked," Raymond said thoughtfully, "what made you take such a leap—from corporate marketing to nonprofit work?"

Vanessa smiled, glancing up at the canopy of fiery-red leaves. "I realized I wasn't living my purpose. Corporate life was comfortable but... empty. I wanted my work to reflect what I believe in—empowering women, strengthening communities, making a real difference."

Raymond nodded, understanding the weight behind her words. "It takes courage to walk away from stability and chase something uncertain."

Vanessa's eyes met his. "It was the best decision I ever made... though it wasn't easy. But sometimes, stepping into the unknown brings the greatest rewards."

Her words resonated deeply with him. He had spent so long cling-ing to the familiar—his role as pastor, his responsibilities as a fa-ther—that he hadn't allowed himself to consider new possibilities.

As they continued walking, their hands brushed briefly, sparking something electric yet tender between them. Neither pulled away.

8

That evening, Raymond returned home, still thinking about Vanes-sa and the quiet peace he felt in her presence. For the first time in years, he allowed himself to consider what life might look like if he dared to let someone in again—not out of loneliness but from a place of genuine connection.

He found himself praying once more, his voice steady but filled with quiet yearning.

"Lord... thank You for the unexpected blessings You've placed in my life. If this is Your will... help me to walk forward without fear."

As he rose from his knees, a sense of clarity washed over him—not certainty of what the future held, but assurance that he was on the right path.

9

Vanessa was equally reflective that evening. As she sat on her apart-ment balcony, wrapped in a soft blanket and cradling a cup of herbal tea, her mind drifted to Raymond—the warmth in his voice, the steadi-ness of his presence. She hadn't planned on opening her heart again, not after the heartbreaks she'd endured in the past.

But Raymond was different—patient, grounded, and unwavering in his faith. He saw the best in people, even when they couldn't see it in themselves.

Her phone buzzed, interrupting her thoughts. It was a message from Raymond:

Raymond: *Thank you for today... for being exactly who you are. I'm grateful for you.*

Vanessa smiled, her heart swelling with an unfamiliar warmth. She typed back:

Vanessa: *I'm grateful for you too... more than you know.*

10

As the weeks went by, Raymond and Vanessa continued building a friendship rooted in mutual respect and shared purpose. They volunteered side by side at community events, exchanged late-night texts about everything from theology to favorite childhood memories, and supported one another through the demands of their respective callings.

One Sunday after service, Raymond invited Vanessa to join him for lunch. They chose a cozy café near the church, settling into a corner booth where they could talk freely.

"I've been thinking..." Raymond began, his voice steady but introspective. "About how God places people in our lives at the right time."

Vanessa smiled softly. "I believe that too. Sometimes we don't realize it until much later."

He met her gaze, his expression open yet cautious. "I don't know what the future holds... but I'm willing to see where this goes—if you are."

Vanessa reached across the table, gently resting her hand on his. "I'm here, Raymond. No rush... no pressure. Let's take it one step at a time."

Relief and hope swelled within him, grounding him in a way he hadn't felt in years.

For the first time in a long while, Raymond allowed himself to believe that new beginnings were possible—not because he was chasing happiness, but because he was finally ready to receive it.

Chapter 13: Collision of Paths

1 Shannon smoothed the front of her dress as she stepped into the sanctuary of Rhema Word Tabernacle. It had been a few weeks since her last visit, and though she wasn't sure what had brought her back today, she felt a pull to be here. Maybe it was the comfort of familiar faces or the chance to see Raymond and Keturah again. Whatever the reason, Shannon had decided to follow that instinct.

The sanctuary buzzed with energy as the congregation greeted one another, laughter and chatter filling the air. Shannon spotted Keturah near the front, sitting with Raymond and some of the church's youth leaders. Her heart warmed at the sight of her daughter, whose face lit up when she noticed her.

"Mommy!" Keturah exclaimed, running over to hug her. "You're here!"

Shannon knelt to embrace her, feeling a wave of gratitude for the joy Keturah brought into her life. "Of course, sweetheart. I wouldn't miss it."

As Keturah pulled her toward the front pews, Shannon glanced up and locked eyes with Raymond. His expression shifted—surprise, then warmth—before he stood to greet her.

"Shannon," he said, his tone welcoming, though a hint of something unreadable lingered in his gaze. "I didn't know you'd be here today."

Shannon smiled, feeling a little self-conscious under his steady gaze. "It was a last-minute decision. I thought it'd be good for Keturah to see us both here."

Raymond nodded, stepping aside to let her sit next to Keturah. As the service began, Shannon couldn't help but feel a sense of nostalgia, a reminder of the life they had once shared. But as her eyes scanned the congregation, they landed on a woman sitting just a few rows back—a woman she didn't recognize.

The woman's attention was fixed on Raymond, her expression warm and engaged. Something about her presence made Shannon's chest tighten, though she quickly brushed the feeling aside, reminding herself that she had no claim on Raymond anymore.

2

After the service, Shannon stayed close to Keturah as they mingled with the congregation. She greeted a few familiar faces, exchanging polite smiles and warm words, but her attention kept drifting back to the woman she had noticed earlier. She was now standing with Raymond, their conversation animated and easy.

Keturah tugged on Shannon's arm, pulling her closer. "Mommy, I want you to meet Miss Vanessa! She's really nice."

Shannon froze for a moment, her mind racing. So this was the woman who had been sitting with such ease in the sanctuary, the one who seemed to share a comfortable rapport with Raymond. Taking a deep breath, she followed Keturah toward them.

Raymond noticed her approach and turned, his expression unreadable but polite. "Shannon, this is Vanessa Carter. She's been working with a local non-profit that partners with the church."

Vanessa extended her hand, her smile bright and genuine. "It's so nice to meet you. Raymond's told me a lot about you."

Shannon hesitated for the briefest of moments before shaking Vanessa's hand, her own smile polite but guarded. "Likewise. Keturah seems to adore you."

Vanessa laughed softly, glancing down at Keturah, who was beaming up at her. "She's an amazing kid. I can see where she gets it from."

The compliment was unexpected, and for a moment, Shannon didn't know how to respond. There was nothing overtly confrontational about Vanessa, yet Shannon couldn't shake the feeling that this woman represented something new, something that had the potential to shift the fragile balance of her relationship with Raymond.

3

As the group moved toward the fellowship hall, Shannon found herself walking beside Vanessa. The conversation was light, focused on the community programs Vanessa was involved in, but Shannon couldn't ignore the subtle undercurrents in their interaction.

"You do a lot of great work," Shannon said, her tone measured. "Rhema Word is lucky to have you."

Vanessa smiled, her gaze steady. "Thank you. It's been a privilege to work with Raymond and the congregation. The community here is incredible."

Shannon nodded, though her thoughts were far from the words being exchanged. She wondered how long Vanessa had been a part of Raymond's life, how close they had become, and whether Keturah's glowing endorsement meant that Vanessa was more than just a professional acquaintance.

"Are you planning to stay involved long-term?" Shannon asked, her voice casual, though the question carried more weight than she let on.

Vanessa tilted her head slightly, sensing the subtext but choosing not to address it directly. "I hope so. There's a lot of potential here, and I feel like I've found a place where I can really make a difference."

Shannon forced a smile, her mind swirling with emotions she couldn't quite name. She had moved on—or at least, she was trying to—but seeing Vanessa here, so integrated into Raymond's life, stirred feelings she thought she had left behind.

4

Later, as Shannon prepared to leave, she found herself lingering near the entrance of the sanctuary, watching as Raymond and Vanessa spoke with a group of church members. Keturah was by her side, chatting happily about the day's events, oblivious to the tension Shannon felt building within her.

When Raymond finally broke away from the group, he approached Shannon, his expression thoughtful. "Thank you for coming today. It meant a lot to Keturah—and to me."

Shannon nodded, her smile faint. "It was good to be here. Keturah loves it when we're all together."

Raymond hesitated, his gaze searching hers. "I hope you know that, no matter what, you'll always be a part of this. For Keturah's sake, and because of everything we've shared."

Shannon swallowed hard, her emotions threatening to overwhelm her. "I know, Raymond. And I feel the same way."

Their conversation was interrupted by Vanessa's approach, her expression warm but cautious. "Shannon, it was really nice meeting you. I hope we'll see you around more often."

Shannon met Vanessa's gaze, forcing herself to respond graciously. "You too, Vanessa. I'm sure we'll be seeing more of each other."

As Shannon left with Keturah, she couldn't help but feel a mix of emotions—gratitude for the time she had spent with her daughter and Raymond, but also a deep uncertainty about where she fit in this evolving dynamic. Vanessa was poised, confident, and clearly cared for by both Raymond and Keturah, and Shannon couldn't ignore the subtle but undeniable tension that their meeting had sparked

5

That evening, as Shannon sat in her living room, she replayed the events of the day in her mind. She thought about Vanessa—her composure, her connection with Raymond, and the ease with which she seemed to fit into the world Shannon had once called her own.

But as much as she felt threatened, she also knew that the path forward wasn't about competition or comparison. It was about clarity—about deciding what she wanted for herself and for Keturah, and whether her future still had a place for Raymond, or if it was time to truly let go.

With a deep breath, Shannon whispered a quiet prayer. "Lord, give me the strength to let go of what's not meant for me and to embrace whatever You have planned. Help me to walk this path with grace, no matter where it leads."

As the night wore on, Shannon felt a sense of calm wash over her. She didn't have all the answers, but she knew she was ready to face whatever came next, trusting that God's plan would guide her steps.

Chapter 14: The Weight of Decisions

1 Shannon couldn't sleep that night. The meeting with Vanessa had been playing in her mind on a loop, each moment replaying itself with unnerving clarity—the warmth in Vanessa's smile, the ease in her voice, the natural connection she seemed to have with Raymond. There hadn't been any overt hostility, but the unspoken tension between them had been impossible to ignore.

Shannon sat up in bed, wrapping a blanket around herself as she gazed out the window. The city lights twinkled in the distance, their steady glow a stark contrast to the turmoil in her heart. She had come to Rhema Word that morning hoping for clarity, perhaps even a renewed sense of belonging. Instead, she had left with more questions than answers.

Her phone buzzed on the nightstand, and she reached for it, surprised to see a message from Raymond: *Thank you for coming today. It meant a lot to Keturah—and to me.*

Shannon stared at the screen, the weight of his words pressing down on her. She typed a quick response: *It was good to be there. Keturah loves spending time with you.*

But as she set the phone aside, Shannon couldn't ignore the lingering ache in her chest. Seeing Raymond with Vanessa had forced her to confront a reality she hadn't been ready to face—that she might not be the only one with options for moving forward.

2

The following day, Raymond sat in his office at Rhema Word, going over notes for an upcoming leadership meeting. Yet, no matter how hard he tried to focus, his thoughts kept drifting back to Shannon. Her presence at church had caught him off guard, but it was her meeting with Vanessa that had truly unsettled him.

He hadn't expected the two women in his life to cross paths so soon. While he and Vanessa were still in the early stages of their friendship, Raymond couldn't deny the growing connection between them. She brought a sense of calm and clarity to his life, qualities he desperately needed as he navigated the challenges of fatherhood and ministry.

But seeing Shannon with Vanessa had stirred something in him—a mix of nostalgia and longing for the life he had shared with her. He wasn't sure if it was love, guilt, or simply the weight of their shared history, but the feelings refused to be ignored.

"Pastor Johnson?" A voice at the door pulled him from his thoughts. It was Vanessa, holding a folder of documents and smiling warmly. "I hope I'm not interrupting."

Raymond gestured for her to come in, grateful for the distraction. "Not at all. What's on your mind?"

Vanessa sat across from him, placing the folder on his desk. "These are the plans for next month's community outreach event. I thought we could go over them together."

As they reviewed the documents, Raymond found himself relaxing, the ease of their conversation providing a welcome reprieve from his inner turmoil. Vanessa had a way of making things feel manageable, even when the weight of the world seemed to rest on his shoulders.

"Thank you for this," Raymond said as they finished. "Your work has been invaluable to the church."

Vanessa smiled, her gaze meeting his. "I'm happy to help. This place has become like a second home to me."

There was a brief silence, and Raymond felt the urge to address the unspoken topic between them. "I hope yesterday wasn't too uncomfortable—for you or Shannon."

Vanessa's expression softened, her voice measured. "I won't pretend it wasn't a little awkward, but I understand. You and Shannon have a lot of history, and that's not something I take lightly."

Raymond nodded, appreciating her honesty. "I just don't want you to feel like you're stepping into something complicated."

Vanessa leaned forward slightly, her tone gentle but firm. "Raymond, life is complicated. Relationships, even more so. But I'm not afraid of complexity. I just want to make sure we're honest with each other about where we stand."

Her words struck a chord, and Raymond felt a mixture of gratitude and apprehension. He wasn't sure where he stood—not with Shannon, not with Vanessa, not even with himself. But he knew he needed to figure it out, and soon.

3

That evening, Shannon met with Tasha at her apartment, seeking her sister's perspective on the day's events. Tasha, now visibly pregnant and glowing with anticipation, listened intently as Shannon recounted her encounter with Vanessa.

"So, she just... showed up in Raymond's life?" Tasha asked, raising an eyebrow.

"Apparently," Shannon replied, her tone tinged with frustration. "She's working with some non-profit that partners with the church. But it's more than that, Tasha. She's... she's involved. She fits in, and Keturah already adores her."

Tasha leaned back on the couch, studying her sister. "And how does that make you feel?"

Shannon hesitated, her emotions bubbling to the surface. "I don't know. Part of me feels... jealous, I guess. Not because I want to be with

Raymond, but because she's stepping into a space I used to occupy. And she's doing it so effortlessly."

Tasha reached over, placing a hand on Shannon's knee. "Shan, it's okay to feel conflicted. You've been through a lot with Raymond, and it's natural to have mixed feelings. But you need to figure out what you really want—for yourself and for Keturah."

Shannon nodded, grateful for her sister's insight. "I just don't want to make the wrong decision. I don't want to hurt anyone."

Tasha's smile was reassuring. "You'll figure it out, Shan. Just take your time, and don't be afraid to be honest—with yourself, with Raymond, and even with Vanessa, if it comes to that."

4

The next Sunday, Shannon found herself back at Rhema Word, this time with a clearer sense of purpose. She had decided to have a conversation with Raymond, to address the lingering tension and define where they stood.

After the service, she approached him in the fellowship hall, her heart pounding as she spoke. "Raymond, can we talk? Privately?"

He nodded, leading her to a quiet corner of the building. "What's on your mind?"

Shannon took a deep breath, steadying herself. "I've been thinking a lot about... us. About everything that's happened over the past few months."

Raymond's expression was calm, though she could see the flicker of uncertainty in his eyes. "And?"

"And I want to be honest with you," she continued. "I've been feeling conflicted—not just about you, but about Vanessa. Seeing her with you... it brought up things I didn't expect."

Raymond listened intently, his voice gentle when he finally spoke. "Shannon, I care about you. I always will. But I need to know where we stand—what you want. Because I can't keep living in this in-between space."

His words hit her like a wave, the truth of them sinking in. She realized that she had been holding onto the past, afraid to let go but also unwilling to fully embrace it. And now, standing before Raymond, she knew she had to make a choice.

"I want what's best for Keturah," she said finally, her voice trembling. "And I want what's best for us, whatever that looks like."

Raymond nodded, his gaze steady. "Then let's figure it out—together."

5

As Shannon left the church that day, she felt a sense of relief, knowing that she and Raymond had taken a step toward clarity. But as she walked to her car, she noticed Vanessa standing nearby, her expression unreadable.

Vanessa approached her, her voice calm but direct. "Shannon, I know this isn't easy for either of us. But I hope we can find a way to co-exist—for Raymond's sake, and for Keturah's."

Shannon met her gaze, feeling a mix of respect and caution. "I hope so too. But let's be clear—I'm not going anywhere."

Vanessa nodded, her smile faint but genuine. "Neither am I."

The two women stood in silence for a moment before parting ways, each carrying the weight of unspoken truths. And as Shannon drove away, she couldn't help but feel that the journey ahead was only just beginning.

Chapter 15: Uncharted Territory

1 Raymond couldn't shake the conversation with Shannon from his mind. Her words had lingered long after she'd left Rhema Word the previous Sunday: *"I want what's best for Keturah... and for us, whatever that looks like."*

It had felt like the closest thing to closure—or perhaps, a beginning—that they'd had in years. Yet, there were still too many unknowns. What did "us" mean after everything they'd been through? Could he even allow himself to hope for reconciliation when Vanessa was becoming an undeniable presence in his life?

He sighed, running his fingers over his Bible as he sat in his church office late into the evening. The stillness of the sanctuary usually brought him peace, but tonight, it only amplified the storm within him.

The door creaked open, and he looked up to see Deacon Henderson standing in the doorway, his weathered face lined with quiet concern.

"Pastor, you alright? It's nearly midnight."

Raymond managed a tired smile. "Couldn't sleep. Thought I'd pray here for a while."

Henderson nodded slowly, stepping inside. "I know that look. You're wrestling with something."

Raymond exhaled, leaning back in his chair. "I thought I had everything figured out—or at least was learning to let go. But now... I feel stuck again."

Henderson took a seat across from him. "You talking about Shannon?"

Raymond's expression tightened. "And Vanessa. Shannon's back in my life in ways I didn't expect, but Vanessa... she's been a light in a dark season. I don't know where this is going, and I'm not sure how to navigate it."

The deacon's gaze softened. "You know, Pastor... sometimes we ask God for clarity, and He gives us choices instead. You're not going to get a perfect answer tied up with a bow. You'll have to trust your heart—and trust Him to guide it."

Raymond nodded slowly, the deacon's words settling into his spirit like a balm. "Thank you."

"Anytime, Pastor. You're not alone."

As Henderson left, Raymond bowed his head in prayer, asking for wisdom, patience, and courage. He didn't know what tomorrow would bring, but he trusted that God was leading him—one step at a time.

2

Across town, Shannon sat curled up on Tasha's couch, a cup of herbal tea warming her hands as her sister folded baby clothes nearby. The scent of lavender and vanilla candles filled the cozy apartment, wrapping them in a sense of calm.

"You've been quiet all night," Tasha observed, folding a soft yellow onesie. "Still thinking about Raymond?"

Shannon nodded, staring into her tea. "I feel like I'm standing at a crossroads, and whichever way I turn, someone's going to get hurt."

Tasha set the onesie aside, fixing her sister with a gentle but knowing look. "It's not about avoiding hurt, Shannon. It's about being honest—with yourself and with them."

Shannon sighed. "I don't even know what I want. Raymond feels like home... but maybe I'm just holding onto the past because it's familiar."

"And Robert?" Tasha prompted.

"He's steady. Kind. Safe," Shannon admitted. "But I'm not sure if that's enough."

Tasha rested a hand on her sister's knee. "Sometimes, 'safe' isn't what your heart needs. Maybe it's time you stop thinking about what's 'right' or 'easy' and ask yourself where you feel *most alive.*"

Shannon swallowed hard, the truth of Tasha's words settling over her like a heavy blanket. She had been running from her feelings, clinging to practicality, afraid to risk the unknown.

Maybe it was time to stop running.

3

The next day, Vanessa arrived at the community center early to set up for the weekly mentorship meeting. She had spent the morning reflecting on her encounter with Shannon. While their conversation had been civil, she couldn't ignore the unspoken tension between them.

Vanessa was no stranger to complicated dynamics—her work with at-risk women had taught her that life was rarely simple. But this felt different. Personal. Close. And despite her confidence, she couldn't shake the feeling that Shannon would always be a part of Raymond's heart.

As she unpacked the workshop materials, she was startled by the sound of the door opening. She looked up to see Shannon standing in the entrance, looking hesitant but resolute.

"Vanessa," Shannon said, her voice steady. "Can we talk?"

Vanessa nodded slowly, gesturing toward a small seating area near the windows. They sat across from each other, the air thick with unspoken emotions.

"I'm not here to cause trouble," Shannon began, her expression earnest. "I know you care about Raymond, and... I'm trying to figure out where I fit in all of this."

Vanessa studied her for a moment, choosing her words carefully. "I appreciate your honesty. And I'm not here to compete with you, Shannon. I care about Raymond, but I respect that you two share a deep history."

Shannon nodded, her voice softening. "I don't want Keturah caught in the middle of... whatever this is becoming."

"Neither do I," Vanessa agreed. "Maybe... we don't have to be on opposite sides."

The words hung between them, both women considering the possibility of coexistence, though neither was sure what that would look like.

4

Later that week, Raymond received a call from Shannon, asking if he could meet her at the park where they often took Keturah. He arrived just after sunset, finding her seated on a bench near the pond, her expression thoughtful.

"Thanks for meeting me," Shannon said as he approached.

Raymond nodded, taking a seat beside her. "Of course. What's on your mind?"

Shannon hesitated, gathering her thoughts. "I've been doing a lot of thinking—about us, about the future... about everything."

His chest tightened, though he kept his expression neutral. "And?"

"I don't know where this path is leading," she admitted. "But I know I don't want to live in the past anymore. I want us to be honest with each other, even if it's hard."

Raymond exhaled slowly, relief and apprehension mixing in his chest. "I want that too."

They sat in silence for a moment, watching the ripples on the water as the breeze stirred the surface. For the first time in a long time, the air between them felt clear—not free of pain or history, but open to possibility.

"I'm willing to try," Shannon said at last, her voice steady. "But I need to know if you are too."

Raymond met her gaze, his voice resolute. "I am."

The past couldn't be rewritten, but the future was still unwritten. And for the first time, they were ready to face it—together.

Chapter 16: A Mother's Choice

1 Tasha paced the small nursery she had carefully prepared, cradling her newborn son, Malachi, in her arms. His tiny face was peaceful as he slept, his chest rising and falling with each soft breath. She gently adjusted the blanket around him, marveling at how something so small could hold her entire world in his grasp.

It had been three weeks since she'd brought Malachi home, and while motherhood came with sleepless nights and endless responsibilities, Tasha found herself embracing every moment. Still, the weight of the unknown loomed heavily—especially when it came to Walter.

He had been calling more frequently, asking about Malachi, expressing a desire to be involved. But promises were easy to make. Showing up was something else entirely. After all the broken commitments and empty apologies, Tasha couldn't ignore the nagging doubt that he wouldn't stay the course.

A soft knock at the door pulled her from her thoughts. She opened it to find Shannon standing there, holding a bag of groceries and flashing a warm smile.

"Thought you could use a restock," Shannon said, stepping inside.

Tasha smiled gratefully. "You're a lifesaver."

Shannon set the groceries on the kitchen counter and turned to face her sister. "How are you holding up?"

Tasha exhaled, leaning against the counter. "I'm... managing. But Walter keeps calling. He says he wants to be part of Malachi's life."

Shannon's expression softened. "Do you believe him?"

"I want to," Tasha admitted, glancing toward the nursery. "But what if he lets us down again? What if Malachi grows up waiting for a father who never shows up?"

Shannon reached for her sister's hand. "You're stronger than you think, Tasha. Whatever you decide, you're not doing this alone."

2

Later that evening, after Shannon had left, Tasha sat on the edge of her bed, scrolling through the messages Walter had sent. His most recent text was still unread: *I need to see Malachi. Please give me a chance.*

She knew she couldn't ignore the situation forever. If she denied Walter the chance to know his son, she risked making a decision she might regret. But if she let him in and he disappeared again, the heartbreak would be unbearable—for her and for Malachi.

Before she could second-guess herself, she typed a response: *We can talk. Tomorrow at noon. The park by my apartment.*

Her finger hovered over the "Send" button, uncertainty gripping her chest. But then she thought of Malachi—his tiny hands, his trusting eyes—and hit "Send."

3

The next day, Tasha arrived at the park early, settling on a bench near the playground. The afternoon breeze rustled the trees, carrying the sounds of children's laughter and birdsong. Malachi stirred lightly in his stroller but remained asleep, his face serene.

She spotted Walter approaching from across the field, his expression a mixture of nervousness and determination. He looked different—cleaner, more put-together—but Tasha had seen transformations like this before. Words and appearances were temporary; actions were what mattered.

"Hey," Walter greeted her cautiously, stuffing his hands into his jacket pockets. "Thanks for meeting me."

Tasha nodded, keeping her expression neutral. "I figured it was time."

His gaze dropped to the stroller, emotion flashing across his face. "Is that...?"

"Malachi," she confirmed, her voice steady. "He's sleeping."

Walter exhaled slowly, his eyes shining with emotion. "I've thought about this moment every day. He's... perfect."

Tasha crossed her arms, unwilling to let sentiment cloud her judgment. "You say you want to be involved. But being a father isn't just showing up when it's convenient, Walter. It's a lifetime commitment."

"I know," Walter said, meeting her gaze earnestly. "I'm not the same man I was before. I've been going to counseling, working steady hours. I'm trying, Tasha. I just want a chance to prove it."

His sincerity was disarming, but Tasha had learned the hard way that sincerity didn't equal stability. "I can't make promises, Walter. Malachi's well-being comes first. If you want to be in his life, you'll have to show me—not just today, but every day."

Walter nodded, emotion thick in his voice. "I will. I swear."

4

The following weeks passed in a blur of sleepless nights, doctor's appointments, and endless diaper changes. To Tasha's surprise, Walter kept his word. He came by regularly, helping with feedings and even attending a parenting class she'd signed up for.

One evening, after putting Malachi to sleep, Tasha found herself sitting across from Walter at her kitchen table, sharing a quiet meal. They talked about work, parenting, and their lives—carefully avoiding the topic of their complicated past.

As he helped clear the table, Walter paused, his expression serious. "Tasha... I know I hurt you. And I know I don't deserve your trust yet. But I'm not going anywhere."

Her throat tightened at the sincerity in his voice. "It's not about deserving, Walter. It's about being consistent."

"I will be," he promised.

For the first time, Tasha allowed herself to believe that maybe, just maybe, he meant it.

5

One month later, Tasha sat in her attorney's office, filling out custody paperwork. The forms felt heavy in her hands, each line a reminder of how much had changed—and how much was still uncertain.

Her lawyer, a sharp but compassionate woman named Olivia Mason, reviewed the documents carefully. "Are you sure about this arrangement?" she asked. "It gives Walter joint custody after a six-month probationary period, contingent on consistent involvement."

Tasha nodded slowly. "I'm sure. He's shown up every day—for Malachi, for me. I can't punish him for his past forever."

Olivia gave her a small, approving smile. "It's a fair arrangement. You're doing what's best for your son."

Tasha exhaled, feeling both relief and apprehension. She knew this wasn't a guarantee, but it was a step toward something better—for Malachi and for herself.

6

That night, as Tasha rocked Malachi to sleep, she whispered a prayer over him:

"Lord, thank You for this precious gift. Help me be the mother he deserves, and give me the strength to make the right choices—even when they're hard. Guide Walter's steps, and let him be the father Malachi needs. And if this path is Your will... give me peace in the journey."

As Malachi's breathing slowed into a steady rhythm, Tasha felt something she hadn't felt in a long time—hope.

For the first time, she believed that their family, broken as it had once been, might be on the verge of healing.

Chapter 17: Caught in the Crossfire

1 Raymond sat in his church office, staring blankly at the sermon notes he'd been working on for hours. The words blurred together, lost in the haze of his restless thoughts. No matter how hard he tried to focus on preparing for Sunday's message, his mind kept circling back to Shannon... and Vanessa.

He had thought time would make things clearer, that the path forward would reveal itself. But instead, he found himself standing at a crossroads, caught between two remarkable women who represented different parts of his heart—and his past and future.

A gentle knock at the door broke his reverie. "Come in," he called, already knowing who it was.

Vanessa stepped inside, her warm smile dimmed by the hint of concern in her eyes. "You missed our planning meeting," she said gently, closing the door behind her. "I wanted to check in."

Raymond sighed, rubbing the back of his neck. "I lost track of time... I've just been distracted."

Vanessa studied him carefully, taking a seat across from him. "Is it Shannon?"

He froze, caught off guard by her directness, though he knew Vanessa wouldn't dance around the truth. She never did.

"I'm trying to figure things out," he admitted. "You and I... we've built something special. But Shannon and I... we have history."

Vanessa nodded slowly, her expression thoughtful but unreadable. "Raymond, I've never asked you to choose. I knew what I was stepping into when we met."

"But that's not fair to you," he countered, his voice tight. "You deserve someone who's all in... someone who doesn't come with this much baggage."

Vanessa's gaze softened. "We all have baggage, Raymond. But you have to figure out what you *want*, not what you think is right—or what you feel obligated to do."

Her words hit home, and Raymond felt a wave of guilt and gratitude all at once. "I don't want to hurt you."

Vanessa smiled faintly, though sadness lingered in her eyes. "Sometimes, love means risking hurt. But you can't stand still forever."

2

Across town, Shannon was preparing for dinner with Robert. Their relationship had grown steadily, though it remained overshadowed by the unresolved feelings she carried for Raymond. She couldn't deny that Robert was stable, attentive, and patient—everything she thought she needed. But her heart still pulled her in two directions.

As she adjusted her necklace in the mirror, her phone buzzed with a message from Raymond: *Can we talk soon?*

Her breath hitched, her fingers hovering over the screen. She typed a quick response: *I'm free tomorrow. Let me know when.*

Setting the phone aside, she exhaled slowly, forcing herself to focus on the evening ahead. Robert deserved her full attention—especially after everything he had patiently endured.

Dinner with Robert went smoothly—almost too smoothly. He was charming and attentive as always, recounting stories from his latest work project. But as the evening wore on, Shannon found herself distracted, caught in a tug-of-war between comfort and longing.

"You seem far away tonight," Robert observed gently, reaching across the table to cover her hand with his.

Shannon met his gaze, guilt twisting in her chest. "I'm sorry... it's just been a long day."

His expression softened, though there was a hint of something guarded in his eyes. "Is it Raymond?"

The question startled her, though she should have expected it. "Robert—"

"I'm not accusing you of anything," he interrupted calmly. "But I know he's still in your life... and in your heart."

Shannon's voice faltered. "He's Keturah's father. He'll always be in my life."

"But what about your heart?" Robert pressed, his voice quiet but insistent. "Is there still room for me?"

Shannon felt tears prick her eyes, her emotions spiraling. "I don't know... I care about you, Robert. But I can't pretend that part of me doesn't still feel connected to him."

His hand tightened around hers, though his voice remained steady. "I can handle complicated, Shannon. But I can't be second place."

3

The next afternoon, Shannon met Raymond at the park where they often took Keturah. He was waiting by the benches, his hands in his pockets, his expression unreadable but earnest.

"Thanks for coming," he said as she approached.

Shannon nodded, her heart pounding. "You said you needed to talk."

Raymond gestured for her to sit, his voice calm but heavy. "I've been doing a lot of thinking... about us, about the future."

Her breath hitched. "And?"

"I'll always care about you, Shannon," he said carefully. "But I don't want to live in the past anymore. We've both changed... and maybe that's okay."

Shannon stared at him, struggling to process his words. "Are you saying... you're done?"

"I'm saying I can't keep holding on to something that might never happen," he replied honestly. "I want us to be good parents. I want us to be friends. But if we can't be more than that... I have to accept it."

His voice trembled slightly at the end, and Shannon felt her chest tighten. "I don't know what I want, Raymond. I thought I did, but—"

"It's okay," he interrupted gently. "You don't have to explain."

Their eyes met, and for a moment, everything they'd been through hung between them—every shared memory, every wound, every hope.

And just like that, the tide shifted.

4

Later that week, Raymond invited Vanessa to dinner at his home—his way of showing her that he was ready to stop standing still. As they prepared a simple meal together, Vanessa seemed more at ease than he had ever seen her, though there was still caution in her eyes.

As they sat together, Raymond reached across the table, covering her hand with his. "I don't have everything figured out... but I want to try—with you."

Vanessa's breath hitched, her eyes shimmering with unshed tears. "Are you sure?"

Raymond nodded firmly. "I'm sure."

For the first time, Vanessa allowed herself to hope—not just for something real, but something lasting.

5

Meanwhile, Shannon sat alone in her apartment, staring at her phone. She knew she couldn't keep Robert waiting. He deserved more than half-hearted affection.

With trembling hands, she dialed his number. "Robert... we need to talk."

His voice was calm, though she could hear the tension beneath it. "I figured this was coming."

"I care about you," she whispered. "But... my heart's not where it needs to be."

Robert exhaled slowly. "Thank you for being honest."

As the call ended, Shannon felt an unfamiliar sense of relief—tinged with sadness but clear, finally.

Chapter 18: Shannon's Plan

1 Shannon paced the length of her living room, her mind racing with possibilities. For the first time in months, she felt a sense of clarity—one that scared and excited her in equal measure. She was done living in the shadows of indecision, done letting the past dictate her future.

She wanted Raymond back.

But wanting him wasn't enough. She needed to show him that she was ready—not just for reconciliation, but for something real and lasting. That meant being honest about her feelings, confronting the pain they'd caused each other, and being willing to fight for what they once had—if there was still something left to fight for.

With renewed determination, she grabbed a notebook from the coffee table and started writing down a plan. Not a manipulative strategy, but a list of honest, intentional steps—ways to rebuild trust, heal old wounds, and remind Raymond of the love that had never truly faded.

At the top of the page, she wrote three words in bold letters: **Be Vulnerable.**

2

The next Sunday, Shannon attended service at Rhema Word—not out of obligation, but because she needed to be where Raymond was. She sat near the back, blending in with the congregation as she listened to him preach about *new beginnings and second chances*.

His words pierced her heart, and she couldn't help but wonder if God was speaking directly to her. She bowed her head, whispering a quiet prayer.

Lord, if there's still a chance for us... show me how to fix what's broken.

After the service, she lingered near the fellowship hall, waiting until most of the congregation had left. As Raymond wrapped up a conversation with Deacon Henderson, she approached cautiously, her pulse quickening.

"Raymond," she called softly.

He turned, surprise flashing in his eyes before his expression settled into something unreadable. "Shannon... I didn't know you'd be here."

She managed a small smile. "I needed to hear today's message."

His gaze softened. "I'm glad you came."

They stood in awkward silence for a moment before Shannon gathered her courage. "Would you be open to having coffee with me sometime? Just... to talk."

Raymond hesitated but finally nodded. "Alright. Let me know when."

Relief washed over her, though she knew this was only the first step. "Thank you."

3

Three days later, they met at a small coffee shop they used to frequent during their early years together. The familiarity of the place brought back bittersweet memories, but Shannon pushed them aside, determined to focus on the present.

They found a quiet table near the window, and for a moment, neither of them spoke. Raymond studied her with cautious curiosity, waiting for her to explain why she'd asked him here.

"I owe you an apology," Shannon began, her voice steady despite the nervous pounding of her heart. "I've been holding back for a long time... afraid to be honest—with you, with myself."

Raymond's expression remained guarded, though she could see the flicker of emotion in his eyes. "What changed?"

Shannon exhaled slowly. "I realized that I've been running from the past instead of facing it. And the truth is... I still love you."

His breath hitched, though he quickly masked his reaction. "Shannon—"

"Wait," she interrupted gently. "I'm not asking for anything... not yet. I just needed you to know how I feel."

He nodded slowly, his voice quiet but sincere. "I appreciate that. But... I'm seeing Vanessa."

Shannon felt the sting of his words but forced herself to stay composed. "I know. And I respect that. But if there's still a part of you that wonders... about us... I'm willing to fight for another chance."

Her honesty left him momentarily speechless. After a long pause, he spoke, his tone thoughtful but careful. "Shannon... I never stopped caring about you. But caring isn't the same as trust."

"I know," she admitted. "But trust can be rebuilt... if you're willing."

Raymond leaned back, studying her with a mixture of longing and uncertainty. "I need time... and honesty—on both sides."

Shannon nodded, her heart swelling with hope. "Then let's start there."

4

Over the next few weeks, Shannon took every opportunity to show Raymond that she was serious—not through grand gestures, but through small, consistent actions.

She volunteered at Rhema Word's community outreach programs, helped organize Keturah's school fundraiser, and even worked alongside Vanessa during church events—despite the lingering awkwardness between them.

Vanessa remained polite but distant, clearly sensing Shannon's intentions. They exchanged few words beyond what was necessary, but there was an unspoken understanding that they were both fighting for the same man—each in their own way.

One Saturday, after a particularly long day of volunteering, Vanessa approached Shannon outside the church, her expression unreadable.

"You're not giving up, are you?" she asked bluntly.

Shannon met her gaze, her voice steady. "No. I'm not."

Vanessa nodded, though her jaw clenched slightly. "Then may the best woman win."

5

One evening, after a long church planning meeting, Raymond found himself walking Shannon to her car. The sun was setting, casting a warm glow over the quiet parking lot.

"You've been... different lately," he admitted, his tone thoughtful. "More open... more like the woman I fell in love with."

Shannon smiled softly. "I'm still her... just a little more broken. But I'm working on that."

He nodded, his expression unreadable but softer than before. "I've noticed."

They stood in silence, the air between them charged with unspoken words.

"Raymond," she whispered, her voice trembling with vulnerability. "I'm not asking you to forget the past... but maybe we can build something new."

His gaze held hers, searching for something—perhaps sincerity, perhaps hope. After a long moment, he spoke quietly:

"I don't know what the future holds... but I'm willing to see where this goes."

Tears stung Shannon's eyes as she nodded, relief and gratitude washing over her. "That's all I'm asking."

As they parted ways, Shannon felt something she hadn't felt in years—*possibility*.

The road ahead would be complicated, and trust wouldn't be re-built overnight. But for the first time, she believed there was still a chance—*their* chance.

And she wasn't going to let it slip away again.

Chapter 19: The Truth Revealed

1 Tasha sat in the dimly lit kitchen, rocking Malachi gently in her arms. His soft coos filled the quiet space, his tiny fingers grasping hers with a strength that always amazed her. Tonight, however, her mind was far from the warmth of motherhood—it was consumed by the upcoming meeting with Walter's parents, Pastors Gerald and Evelyn Grant.

It had been Walter's idea. After months of trying to rebuild his relationship with her and Malachi, he insisted that they meet with his parents, believing it was time to address the past—their absence, the strained silence, and the secrets that had driven them apart.

Tasha had agreed, but only reluctantly. Walter's parents had always been a towering presence in his life, and their disapproval of her had loomed over their relationship like an unforgiving storm. She hadn't seen or spoken to them since the early days of her pregnancy, when their sharp words and harsh judgments had left scars she still carried.

Now, they wanted to meet at the church. Neutral ground, Walter had said. But to Tasha, it felt like walking into the lion's den.

"Lord," she whispered, her voice trembling, "help me be strong—for Malachi's sake."

2 The next afternoon, Tasha arrived at Living Truth Ministries, where Pastors Gerald and Evelyn had served faithfully for decades. The church was imposing, with its towering steeple and carefully manicured grounds—a symbol of legacy, authority, and tradition.

Walter was already waiting outside, pacing near the front steps. His face lit up when he saw her, though his smile dimmed slightly when he noticed her tense posture.

"You didn't have to come alone," he said, opening the car door to help her lift Malachi's car seat.

Tasha shrugged, keeping her voice steady. "This is between us. No need to involve anyone else."

Walter nodded, his expression unreadable. He led her into the church's large meeting hall, where his parents were waiting.

Pastor Gerald stood near the long oak table, his imposing frame radiating authority, while Evelyn sat primly at the far end, her expression guarded but composed. Tasha felt a familiar chill settle over her—a reminder of all the times she had stood in this room feeling judged, unwanted, and less-than.

"Tasha," Evelyn said stiffly, offering a thin, practiced smile. "Thank you for coming."

Tasha nodded, cradling Malachi instinctively. "Pastor Evelyn. Pastor Gerald."

Walter cleared his throat. "I thought it was time we all talked—really talked."

3

The meeting began awkwardly, with formal pleasantries and surface-level questions about Malachi's health and milestones. But Tasha could feel the tension building beneath the polite facade, like a river ready to burst its banks.

Finally, she couldn't hold back any longer. "Why now?" she demanded, her voice sharper than she intended. "You never showed up when I was pregnant. You judged me... left me to figure everything out alone. And now, after all this time, you want to be involved?"

Gerald's jaw tightened, but it was Evelyn who spoke first. "We didn't handle things the way we should have," she admitted, though her tone remained formal. "But we had our reasons."

Tasha crossed her arms, meeting her gaze head-on. "Then explain them."

Evelyn exchanged a look with her husband before continuing. "We... didn't believe Walter was ready to be a father. He was still struggling, still... lost."

"That's not your call to make," Tasha snapped. "I deserved to know what was going on—not be left in the dark while you decided what was best for me and my child."

Gerald finally spoke, his deep voice steady but strained. "We were trying to protect you—from him and from the instability we saw in his life at the time."

Their words landed heavily, though they did little to soothe the ache in Tasha's chest. "You thought you were doing what was best," she said bitterly. "But you took away his choice—and mine."

4

Walter stepped forward, his voice tight with emotion. "Mom, Dad... you should've told me Tasha reached out back then. You should've let me figure it out."

Evelyn's face softened, guilt flashing in her eyes. "You were in no condition to be anyone's father, Walter. We thought we were sparing her more pain."

Walter shook his head, his voice breaking. "I *wanted* to be there... even if I didn't know how. You had no right to take that away."

Tasha swallowed hard, her anger warring with a deep, weary sadness. "I could've handled the truth... even if it hurt. But being shut out—that hurt more than anything."

For the first time, Gerald's imposing facade cracked, his shoulders sagging under the weight of regret. "We were wrong," he admitted quietly. "We let our fear control us... and we failed you both."

Tasha's breath hitched, emotion rising in her throat. After all these years, after all the pain and confusion, hearing those words felt like both a relief and a fresh wound.

5

Silence settled over the room, thick with unresolved history. After what felt like an eternity, Evelyn rose from her seat and approached Tasha cautiously.

"I know we can't undo the past," she said softly. "But we'd like to be part of Malachi's life... if you'll let us."

Tasha blinked back tears, her grip tightening on Malachi's tiny hand. "It's not about what *I* want... it's about what's best for him."

Gerald stepped forward, his voice trembling. "We want to do right by him—and by you."

Walter reached for Tasha's hand, his touch warm and steady. "We can figure this out... together."

Tasha nodded slowly, her heart still heavy but no longer closed. "We'll try."

It wasn't forgiveness—not yet. But it was a start.

6

That night, Tasha knelt beside Malachi's crib, whispering a quiet prayer.

"Lord... help me let go of the past. Give me the strength to forgive—not just for them, but for myself. And help us build something new—for Malachi, and for all of us."

As she rose, she felt lighter—not because the pain was gone, but because she had finally stopped carrying it alone.

The journey toward healing had only just begun—but for the first time, she believed it was possible.

Chapter 20: Breaking Point

1 The sanctuary of Rhema Word Tabernacle buzzed with activity as volunteers prepared for the church's annual community gala—a night of celebration, testimony, and fundraising. Raymond stood near the front of the fellowship hall, directing last-minute logistics, though his mind was far from the event.

For weeks, the growing tension between Shannon and Vanessa had been an unspoken undercurrent in his life. Despite his best efforts to compartmentalize, he couldn't deny that a reckoning was coming—one he could no longer avoid.

As if summoned by his thoughts, he saw Shannon enter, wearing a deep blue dress that accentuated her graceful presence. His breath caught, memories of their shared past rushing to the forefront. Before he could greet her, Vanessa appeared from the other side of the hall, clipboard in hand, exuding quiet confidence as she coordinated with volunteers.

Two powerful presences. Two lives tangled with his in ways he could no longer ignore.

"Pastor Raymond?" Deacon Henderson called, pulling him from his thoughts. "We're ready for the opening prayer."

Raymond nodded, steadying himself. He could handle the gala—but what came after felt far less certain.

2
The gala unfolded smoothly, the atmosphere warm and celebratory. Vanessa, ever the organized leader, managed the flow of the evening

with practiced ease, ensuring that every detail went according to plan. Shannon, meanwhile, worked quietly behind the scenes, assisting wherever she could while keeping a watchful eye on Raymond.

Despite the distance they tried to maintain, it was impossible to ignore the lingering glances, the silent acknowledgments charged with meaning.

As the evening progressed, Raymond took the stage to deliver a heartfelt message about community and grace. His voice was steady, but his words carried an intensity rooted in his personal struggles—his search for clarity, for purpose, for resolution.

When he concluded, the room erupted into applause, but Shannon and Vanessa's gazes remained fixed on him, each silently wondering where his heart truly lay.

3

Later that evening, as the gala wound down, Raymond stepped outside for some air, the cool night breeze a welcome reprieve from the intensity of the evening. He closed his eyes, savoring the brief moment of solitude—until the sound of approaching footsteps pulled him back to reality.

He turned to find Shannon standing a few feet away, her expression uncertain but determined.

"Raymond... can we talk?" she asked softly.

Before he could respond, the door opened again, and Vanessa emerged, stopping short when she saw them. Tension crackled like electricity in the air.

"I didn't mean to interrupt," Vanessa said, her tone calm but clipped. "I was just checking on the cleanup."

Shannon squared her shoulders. "You're not interrupting. This won't take long."

Raymond held up a hand, his voice strained. "Maybe we should all talk."

Vanessa's eyebrows rose, her posture rigid. "Is that what you want?"

Shannon's gaze remained steady. "I'm done avoiding this."

4

The three of them moved toward the quiet garden behind the church, far from the lingering guests. The air between them was thick with unresolved emotions, every unspoken word threatening to spill over.

"I'm tired of pretending this isn't happening," Shannon began, her voice trembling but firm. "I still love you, Raymond. I've never stopped. And I'm done standing on the sidelines while we tiptoe around the truth."

Vanessa inhaled sharply but kept her composure. "I see," she said evenly. "So, this is your way of reclaiming what you walked away from?"

Shannon's eyes flashed with hurt. "I didn't walk away. We *both* failed—but I'm here now, trying to fix what we lost."

Raymond ran a hand through his hair, frustration etched into his features. "This isn't about who's right or wrong—"

"No," Vanessa interrupted, her voice sharp. "But it *is* about what you want, Raymond. You can't keep living in the past and the present at the same time."

His shoulders sagged under the weight of her words. "I didn't ask for any of this to happen."

Vanessa's expression softened, though her voice remained steady. "I know... but you still have to choose."

5

For a moment, there was only silence—thick, oppressive, and unyielding. Raymond felt as though the weight of the entire world rested on his chest. He cared for Vanessa—her steadiness, her heart, her belief in him when he'd doubted himself the most. But Shannon...

Shannon was a part of his soul, tangled in memories of love, hurt, forgiveness, and unfinished promises.

"I never meant to hurt either of you," he said finally, his voice hoarse. "But I can't keep pretending this isn't tearing all of us apart."

Shannon took a shaky breath. "Then be honest—with us and with yourself."

Raymond's gaze lingered on Vanessa, her expression a mix of strength and sorrow. "Vanessa... you've been my anchor when I needed one the most. You've shown me what grace looks like, even when I didn't deserve it."

Her eyes glistened, but she remained silent, giving him the space he needed.

Then he turned to Shannon, emotion threatening to overwhelm him. "And you... you were my first love. My greatest joy... and my deepest heartbreak."

His voice trembled, thick with emotion. "I don't know where this road leads... but I know where my heart keeps returning."

Shannon's breath hitched, tears spilling down her cheeks as hope sparked in her chest.

Vanessa exhaled slowly, her face etched with understanding and heartbreak. "I see."

6

The weight of the moment settled heavily on all of them. Vanessa stepped forward, lifting her chin with quiet dignity. "I won't stand in the way of what's meant to be."

Raymond opened his mouth to speak, but she gently placed a hand on his arm, stopping him. "Thank you... for being honest."

With that, she turned and walked back toward the church, her silhouette fading into the dim light of the sanctuary.

Shannon stood frozen, still reeling from what had just happened. "Raymond... are you sure?"

He nodded slowly, his voice steady despite the storm raging within. "I'm sure."

For the first time in what felt like forever, Shannon allowed herself to believe that redemption, forgiveness, and second chances might still be possible.

But as they stood together under the quiet, starlit sky, Raymond couldn't shake the lingering ache in his chest—a reminder that even the right choices often come with a cost.

Chapter 21: Healing Begins

1 The following Sunday, the air at Rhema Word Tabernacle was thick with expectation. Word of Raymond's personal decision had quietly spread among the church's leadership, though no formal announcements had been made. Those closest to him knew that change was coming—not just for the pastor, but for the entire congregation.

Raymond stood in his office, staring out the window as the morning sun bathed the church grounds in a soft, forgiving light. His decision to be with Shannon still weighed heavily on his heart—not because he regretted it, but because of the unavoidable pain it caused Vanessa.

He heard a soft knock at the door and turned to see Shannon standing in the doorway, her expression tentative but hopeful. She wore a simple dress that reflected her new outlook: grounded, hopeful, and unguarded.

"Hey," she said softly.

"Hey."

They stood in silence for a moment before Shannon stepped inside, resting her hand gently on his arm. "Are you ready?"

Raymond exhaled slowly, placing his hand over hers. "As ready as I'll ever be.

2

The sanctuary was packed, buzzing with quiet conversations that stilled as Raymond approached the pulpit. His heart pounded as he adjusted the microphone, taking a steadying breath before speaking.

"Good morning, Rhema Word," he began, his voice steady but laced with emotion. "Today's message is about grace… not just the grace we receive from God, but the grace we extend to one another."

His gaze swept across the congregation, pausing briefly on Shannon, who sat near the front with Keturah, her expression steady with quiet strength. Then, his eyes shifted to the back row, where Vanessa sat alone, her face serene but resolute.

"We are all on a journey," Raymond continued. "We face choices that define us, struggles that refine us, and moments where we have to trust that God's plan is bigger than our understanding."

He paused, emotion tightening his throat. "I stand before you today as someone who has been broken, rebuilt, and shown more grace than I could ever deserve. And I'm here to tell you—there is *always* hope. There is *always* redemption."

The room fell silent, the weight of his words settling over the congregation like a healing balm.

3

After the service, the congregation lingered in quiet conversations, moved by Raymond's message. Shannon and Keturah waited by the entrance, sharing warm greetings with familiar faces as Raymond spoke with church members near the altar.

Vanessa stood quietly near the back, observing the scene with a calm acceptance. She had come today knowing what it would cost her emotionally, but she had refused to let heartache drive her away from a place she now considered home.

As she turned to leave, Raymond caught sight of her and gently excused himself, crossing the room with measured steps.

"Vanessa," he called softly.

She stopped but didn't turn around. "I didn't come for closure, Raymond. I came… because I still belong here."

He nodded slowly. "I'm glad you did. You'll always have a place here… in this church, in this community."

For the first time, her expression softened into something warmer. "I didn't stay because of you... but I'm not leaving because of you either."

Raymond's chest tightened, gratitude and regret mingling in his heart. "Thank you... for everything."

Vanessa offered a faint but genuine smile. "Take care of them—of yourself."

With that, she walked toward the exit, her steps steady, her spirit unbroken.

4

Outside, Vanessa paused near the church's garden, where blooming hydrangeas swayed gently in the breeze. She closed her eyes, whispering a quiet prayer for peace—not just for herself, but for Raymond, for Shannon, and for the journey ahead.

"Vanessa?"

She turned to see Shannon standing a few feet away, hesitant but resolute.

"I wasn't sure if you'd want to talk," Shannon admitted, folding her arms.

Vanessa studied her carefully before nodding. "I'm listening."

Shannon stepped closer, her voice trembling with sincerity. "I know I hurt you... just by being here. I can't undo that. But... I'm grateful for what you've meant to Raymond—and to this church."

Vanessa's expression remained unreadable for a moment before softening. "You don't owe me an apology, Shannon. This... was never about winning or losing. It was about what was meant to be."

"I still hope we can coexist... somehow," Shannon offered cautiously.

Vanessa considered this, her gaze thoughtful. "We already are."

With that, Vanessa extended her hand—not as a rival, but as someone choosing grace over resentment. Shannon accepted it with quiet relief, knowing that forgiveness didn't come easily—but it had come nonetheless.

5

That evening, Raymond, Shannon, and Keturah sat together in their living room, laughter spilling over as they played a board game. It was a simple, unremarkable moment—yet it felt monumental.

Later, after Keturah had gone to bed, Raymond and Shannon sat on the porch, wrapped in a comfortable silence beneath the stars.

"Do you think we can really make this work?" Shannon whispered.

Raymond reached for her hand, lacing his fingers through hers. "I think... we already are."

She smiled, resting her head against his shoulder as peace settled around them—hard-earned, but deeply cherished.

6

At Rhema Word the following Sunday, Vanessa took her usual seat near the back of the sanctuary, her spirit lighter than it had been in months. She no longer felt like an outsider looking in—she belonged, not because of Raymond or anyone else, but because of the calling she felt in her heart.

As the choir sang, Vanessa closed her eyes, lifting her voice in worship. Healing was a process, not a moment—but she was ready for it.

And for the first time in a long time, she felt free—not from the past, but from the weight of holding onto it.

About the Author

About the Author

D. Elias Loadholt Sr. is a passionate storyteller, preacher, and advocate for healing through faith. Known for his authentic voice and deeply relatable teaching style, Dwayne weaves together spiritual insight, emotional honesty, and everyday struggles to reveal the beauty of God's grace in broken places.

A native of Brooklyn, New York now rooted in Midlothian, Virginia, Dwayne has spent years serving in ministry—mentoring youth, building community, and preaching the Gospel with boldness and compassion. His love for storytelling was born in the church pews and sharpened on real-life journeys of pain, resilience, and redemption.

He is a husband to **Charmaine.** Together, they are raising their three incredible children—**Cyarrah, Savannah, and Dwayne Jr.**—who remain his greatest legacy and daily motivation.

Hiding Behind the Cross is his debut novel, a faith-filled exploration of love, loss, healing, and the uncomfortable but necessary work of transformation.

Follow him on social media @bishopdlo in Instagram & Tik Tok. Also @D Elias Loadholt Sr on Facebook for faith-based content, encouragement, and more stories to come.

www.ingramcontent.com/pod-product-compliance
Lightning Source LLC
Chambersburg PA
CBHW071527150726
48000CB00002B/710